WHAT A WEEK TO TAKE A CHANCE

Rosie Rushton lives in Moulton, Northamptonshire. She is a school governor of a new secondary school and in May 2004 was licensed as a Reader in the Church of England. Her hobbies include tracing her family history, travelling the world, being with her grandchildren, walking, theatre, reading and all things Indian. In the future she wants to write a TV drama for teenage audiences, visit Kathmandu, write the novel that has been pounding in her brain for years but has never quite got to the keyboard, and learn to slow down and smell the roses. Her many books for Piccadilly Press include *Break Point*, *Tell Me I'm OK, Really* and several series including Best Friends, The Girls and The Leehampton Quartet.

Coming soon from Piccadilly Press . . .

What a Week Omnibus: Books 1-3
including:
What a Week to Fall in Love
What a Week to Make it Big
What a Week to Break Free

Book 8: *What a Week to Get Real*
Book 9: *What a Week to Risk it All*

ROSIE RUSHTON

Piccadilly Press · London

For Amy Flynn

And with grateful thanks to Hannah Herde
and Year Seven of South Hampstead
High School for Girls GDST

First published in Great Britain in 2004
by Piccadilly Press Ltd.,
5 Castle Road, London NW1 8PR
www.piccadillypress.co.uk

A catalogue record for this book is available from the British Library

ISBN: 185340 880 8 (trade paperback)

1 3 5 7 9 10 8 6 4 2

Printed and bound in Great Britain by Bookmarque Ltd
Text design by Louise Millar. Set in Legacy
Cover illustration by Sue Hellard. Cover design by Fielding Design

MONDAY

7.00 a.m.

53 Lime Avenue, Oak Hill, Dunchester. In Jade's bedroom, sharing problems

'Jade, I've had this amazing idea. Oh, for heaven's sake, you're not asleep, are you?'

Jade Williams rolled over in bed as her door slammed and her cousin Allegra bounded into the room, her long ash-blonde hair flopping over her eyes.

'Fat chance of that, the way you stomp around,' Jade muttered, not wanting to admit that she had been awake for ages working out her life plan. Or lack of it. 'Don't you ever knock?'

'Sorry,' Allegra said, shrugging. She slumped down on the bed. 'Just because you've got your own bedroom now, you don't have to go all prissy on me. Now listen, it's about Scott . . .'

'Why doesn't that surprise me?' Jade muttered, her heart sinking. 'Do you have to keep going on about him?' She felt guilty enough about dumping Scott without having his name shoved down her throat twenty-four/seven.

'I don't keep going on,' retorted Allegra. 'And anyway, what's it to you?' She eyed Jade in alarm. 'You're not having second thoughts?' she demanded. 'I mean, you don't want to get it together with him again?'

Jade sighed. 'How many more times do I have to tell you?' she replied. 'Scott Hamill and me are finished. Over. History. Get it?'

She threw back the duvet and stuffed her feet into her slippers. The last thing she wanted to do was get into a conversation about boys. All her mates might think they were the hot topic; she didn't. Which made her worry that there was something wrong with her.

'If you want him, he's all yours,' she added. 'I'm done with boys.'

Allegra stared at her. 'Get real,' she urged. 'What's life without guys, for heaven's sake?'

'A hell of a lot easier than life with them,' muttered Jade, running her fingers through her tousled hair. 'Now, if you don't mind, I'm going to take a shower.'

She grabbed her bathrobe and headed for the door.

'No, wait!' pleaded Allegra, blocking her path. 'I need your advice.'

Despite her reluctance to think about Scott Hamill, Jade hesitated. Ever since her parents had died and she'd come to live with her aunt, Paula, her uncle, David, and cousins, Allegra and Helen, she had either been totally ignored by her elder cousin, or suffered countless put- downs and sarcastic remarks. It was actually kind of cool to finally be treated with respect.

'Advice about Scott and you, I assume?'

Allegra sighed. 'That's the whole problem,' she complained. 'There is no Scott and me. I don't get it –

I've done all the things you're supposed to do.'

'Like what?'

'You know, pretending to be dumb at French and asking for his help, freezing to death on Sunday mornings watching him play football, sending him sexy text messages and e-cards . . .'

'You didn't?' exclaimed Jade, sinking back down on the bed. 'You are so . . .'

'So what?' demanded Allegra, tossing her head and glaring at Jade. 'Imaginative? Streetwise? Well, I wouldn't expect you to understand those techniques, little Mrs Prim and Proper!'

'Funny thing is,' Jade retorted, flinging open the bedroom door, 'that I'm the one who went out with Scott for weeks and weeks and you're the one he's ignoring. Some technique!'

If it hadn't been for the look of pure desolation that flashed across Allegra's face, Jade would have felt quite proud of her swift comeback. But to her horror, her cousin's eyes filled with tears.

'Sorry, Legs, that was mean,' she said hastily. 'Look, it hasn't been that long since I dumped Scott – maybe he just needs some time to get his head together.'

'I wish!' Allegra moaned. 'It might help if he would stop talking about you all the time. *Do you think Jade will change her mind? Could you talk to Jade for me?* It's vomit-making.'

She glared at Jade. 'I thought he might forget you over

the Christmas holidays, what with him going to the States and everything, but what happens? You get three postcards and two phone calls and I get zilch, zippo, nothing!'

'That's hardly my fault,' Jade protested, not wanting to let on that in fact she had a load of slushy text messages as well. 'It's not like I give the guy any encouragement.'

'Precisely!' Allegra burst out. 'That's it, you see. That's the problem.'

'The *problem*?' Jade queried. 'Last night, you were telling me that in future, if I so much as sit at the same table as Scott in the cafeteria, you would personally tear me limb from limb.'

'Yes, but since then, I've been thinking,' Allegra cut in.

'Now, that's a new experience,' Jade teased.

'Shut it,' retorted Allegra. 'Do you want to help me or not?'

'Yes, of course,' said Jade, with a sigh, knowing that agreement was the only way she was ever going to get near the shower.

'Well,' Allegra went on. 'We've got to get Scott to go off you big time, OK?'

Jade said nothing. She didn't want to go out with Scott; she didn't want him getting all heavy and trying to take over her life – but she did want him to like her. She wanted everyone to like her.

'And I've tried everything,' Allegra went on, running her fingers through her newly-straightened hair. 'I keep telling him that you are really immature . . .'

'Oh thanks!' Jade snapped, jumping up and striding over to the door. 'If I'm so immature you won't need my advice, will you?'

She stomped down the spiral staircase from her attic bedroom to the bathroom on the first floor.

'Jade, wait,' Allegra pleaded, clattering down after her. 'I'm sorry, OK?' She looked so downcast that Jade couldn't help feeling sorry for her.

'Look, I'm sure it will work out, Legs,' she assured her cousin, even though she wasn't sure at all. 'But there's nothing I can do about it.'

'That's where you're wrong,' Allegra burst in excitedly. 'I've got this plan.'

'Please tell me,' said Jade, sighing, 'that it doesn't involve booze, nightclubs . . .'

'Go on, throw all that back in my face,' Allegra stormed. 'So I made mistakes – you can hardly talk. What about running away and . . . ?'

Despite her irritation, Jade couldn't help smiling. 'OK, OK, point taken,' she said, nodding. 'So go on, tell me about the plan. But could you do it in under a minute? I want to wash my hair.'

'You,' announced Allegra triumphantly, 'are going to let Scott think that you want him back.'

'Are you mad?' Jade exploded. 'Two minutes ago, you were going ballistic at the thought of me looking at the guy!'

'That's when I thought you might really want him,' Allegra said dismissively. 'Anyway, listen. It's your birthday on Saturday, right?'

'So?' Jade didn't mean to sound abrupt but the thought of her approaching birthday reminded her of her dead parents and whenever she thought of them, all she wanted to do was cry.

'And you're going to have a party . . .'

'I don't want a party!'

'Don't be silly, everyone wants parties,' retorted Allegra. 'So, starting today, you're going to chat up Scott, phone him . . .'

'No!'

'Give him the idea that he's in with a chance . . .'

'Oh puh-leese!'

'And then you'll invite him to your party and be really, really horrid to him!'

'Why would I do that?'

'Because you don't want him and I do. Face it, Jade – you spend your whole life saying you want to make a difference and help people, right?'

'Yes, but . . .'

'Well, now you don't have to wait to be a nurse in some grotty African village. You can do it right here. For me.'

'Allegra!' Jade shouted, her green eyes flashing with indignation.

'Yes?'

'What part of the word "no" don't you understand?'

7.25 a.m.

6 Kestrel Close, West Green, Dunchester.

Cleo's bedroom – being pestered by a parent

'Cleo! Darling, you're still not dressed!'

Cleo Greenway was in the middle of examining her chin for fresh zits when her bedroom door flew open and her mother, dressed in a crimson kaftan and slippers that would not have been out of place on the set of *Aladdin*, burst into the room.

'Never mind,' her mum gabbled. 'You dress, I'll talk.'

'Mum, can't it wait?' Cleo protested, wrinkling her nose as a cloud of her mother's *Allure* perfume hit her nostrils. 'Have you never heard of privacy?'

'Oh darling, I'm your mother,' Diana Greenway cried dismissively, perching on the end of Cleo's unmade bed. 'Now hurry up, or you'll be late for school. Is that bra getting too small?'

'Mum! If you're going to get personal . . .' Cleo began, cupping her hands over her boobs in embarrassment. Recently her breasts appeared to have taken on a life of their own and swelled to alarming proportions; her friend Holly said she was dead lucky but then Holly didn't have to hump the wretched things around all day.

'Sorry, sorry!' Her mother held up her hands in mock surrender. 'Now listen, there's something I need to discuss with you.'

'Like cutting my allowance, I suppose,' Cleo retorted, pulling her chocolate-brown school trousers over her hips and grappling with the zip. 'Just because you're having an economy drive, I don't see why I should be made to suffer.'

In the past couple of months, her mother, who until recently could have won the title of Shopaholic of the Century, had undergone a personality transplant. Instead of spending money like it was going out of fashion, she had taken to cutting out 'money off' coupons from magazines, scanning charity shops for clothes and - worst of all - cooking meals that didn't come out of packets from Marks and Spencer.

'It won't last,' Portia, Cleo's seventeen-year-old sister had assured her. 'Cheap and cheerful just isn't Mum's style.'

But it *had* lasted. In fact, it had got worse. The evening before, Roy, Cleo's stepfather, had joined in the campaign, declaring that he was cutting everyone's allowance by a third for the next three months.

'For once,' he had announced pompously, pushing his wife's attempt at vegetable lasagne round his plate, 'your mother is making an effort to act like a rational human being. Not before time, I admit.' He had laughed uproariously, but Cleo heard the biting sarcasm behind his remark and hated him for it.

'You can't do that!' Portia had gasped. 'I'm the poorest person at college as it is.'

'While you live under my roof,' Roy had replied, the hairs in his nostril waving indignantly, 'I call the shots.'

'I hate you!' Lettie had shouted, bursting into tears. Lettie, the youngest of the Greenway sisters, was such a baby that everyone ignored her outburst.

'It is high time,' Roy had droned on, 'that this family joined the Real World.'

Roy talked a lot about the Real World. Apparently, it was full of teenagers who always agreed with their parents, preferred homework to MTV and never ditched a garment until it was totally threadbare.

'It's not our fault that Mum's got credit card debts,' Cleo had muttered, somewhat ill-advisedly.

'No,' her stepfather had ranted, 'and it's not her fault that you ran up a mammoth phone bill calling some spotty youth in America!'

She would have leapt to the defence of Trig's skin quality, but she was too busy struggling not to cry. It was nearly five months since Trig had left West Green School to go back to his home in Illinois, and almost two months since he had texted her to say he'd found a new girlfriend. But it still hurt as if it were yesterday. Her friends all told her to forget him and find someone else; which would have been fine, except that there weren't too many guys queuing up to take her out.

'Honestly, Mum,' Cleo insisted now, pulling her blond hair into a pony-tail. 'All my mates get more money than I do and there's Jade's birthday present to get . . .'

'Oh, don't look so worried, cherub,' her mother butted in. 'With a bit of luck, I've got the answer to all our money worries.'

'You have?' Cleo asked. 'Another part?'

It had been some time since Diana Greenway, who many years before had been acclaimed by *The Guardian* newspaper as 'an exciting newcomer to the British stage', had played anything other than the Fairy Queen in *Iolanthe* or a traffic warden in ITV's latest soap.

'Not exactly,' her mum admitted. 'You remember I did that wonderful Fittinix advert for television?'

'How could I ever forget?' Cleo said with a sigh, peering in the mirror at a zit that had appeared overnight. The memory of her mother, clad only in her underwear, floating in a hot air balloon above Dunchester town centre haunted her dreams to this day.

'Well, it would seem I was noticed by an amazing number of people,' her mother went on proudly.

'Hardly surprising,' Cleo muttered under her breath.

'And you will never guess what's happened as a result,' her mother giggled.

'You've been sectioned under the Mental Health Act?' Cleo teased.

'Oh darling, really, you are too funny!' trilled her mother. 'Do I look like a madwoman?'

'Frequently.' Cleo nodded. 'So come on – let's hear the worst. What is it this time?'

'Well,' said her mum, grinning and wriggling her

bottom into a more comfortable position on the end of the bed, 'you know that TV programme? The one where they send people into the rainforest and make them crawl through pits of maggots and stuff?'

Cleo's eyes widened in alarm. 'Not *Jungle Junkets*? Mum, you can't! You scream when a wasp gets into the kitchen.'

Diana pulled a face. 'Well, actually, they did ask me to do it, but I said no,' she told Cleo. 'I said I couldn't bear to be parted from my girls in their formative years, and that's when they got all excited.'

Cleo shook her head and sighed. 'Mum, if you have something to tell me, could you do it in words of one syllable? Quickly?'

'OK, OK.' Her mother nodded. 'These people are going to make a new TV series called *Like Mother, Like Daughter* for that new digital channel everyone's talking about. What's it called?'

'How would I know? We don't have digital – Roy's too tight-fisted.'

'WOW TV, that's it!' her mother exclaimed. 'Anyway, there will be loads of cash prizes, darling – and they want us!'

Cleo's brain went on red alert. 'When you say *us* . . .'

'You and me, darling. Isn't it exciting – you always said you wanted to be on TV.'

'I never said anything of the sort,' Cleo protested, picking up her hairbrush. 'One exhibitionist in our family is quite enough.'

Her mother flicked an imaginary piece of fluff from her sleeve and inspected her fingernails. It was a gesture Cleo knew only too well.

'Of course, if you don't want to help us get out of this wretched financial mess . . .' her mother began. 'I know I've been overspending but I thought we were all pulling together, doing our bit . . .'

Her eyes filled with tears which would have made Cleo feel dreadful had it not been for the fact that her mother could switch her dramatic talents on at a moment's notice if she thought there was something in it for her.

'So what is it?' sighed Cleo, stuffing her coursework folder into her school bag. 'A chat show?'

'No, darling, something far more exciting. They take a whole load of *celebrity* mums . . .' Cleo grinned as her mother emphasised the word 'celebrity'. '. . . and their daughters. They don't let the viewers know which kid goes with which mum. Then they line the daughters up and the viewers have to guess which celebrity goes with which daughter.'

'Riveting,' said Cleo, sighing. 'Is that it?' Watching paint dry would be more exciting, she thought.

'Well, of course there's lots more to it than that,' her mother murmured vaguely. 'Something about the voting for which mother and daughter stay to the next round. And they do challenges – or something like that. I didn't quite understand.'

Cleo sighed. Her mother rarely grasped the details of life.

'Oh, and the kids have to show off their talents – you'd sing, of course, treasure, which would put the audience off the scent because of course singing is one of the few things I can't do and . . .'

'No way, Mum. Absolutely not. Forget it.'

Her mother's face fell. 'But darling, you love to sing,' she began.

'In the school choir, Mum – not on national TV,' Cleo pointed out.

'But there's money in it – lots – and heaven knows we need it.'

'Well, can't Portia or Lettie do it?' Cleo demanded.

'Oh goodness no, darling – Lettie's too young and Portia's too like me – tall, same bone structure, slim, my eyes – everyone would guess she was mine in two seconds flat and we'd be out of the game.' She took Cleo's hand. 'You'd be perfect, you see,' she explained. 'You're not a bit like me – your colouring's all different, you're slightly podgy – you get that from your father, of course – you're a bit on the shy side, you've got that Dunchester twang to your voice . . .'

'I so have not!'

'And you're not one these beauty-obsessed, fashion-mad kids . . .'

'Oh, great!' shouted Cleo. 'So I'm the ugly, overweight, boring-looking one, right? I'm the one that you can sigh over and say stuff like "I don't know where

she gets her spots from – I've never had a zit in my life!"'
She grabbed her school bag and swallowed hard as she yanked open the bedroom door.

'Darling, I didn't mean it to come out like that,' her mother pleaded. 'What I meant was . . .'

'Mum, forget it, OK? Reality TV stinks, anyway. Mrs Bewley said that it's demeaning, intrusive . . .'

'But darling, you have to give the viewing public what they want,' her mother insisted.

'No, Mum. I don't have to give them anything. You do what you like – but count me out.'

'But Cleo, why?' her mother begged, following her down the stairs.

'Because it goes against all my moral and ethical principles,' she retorted, recalling the phrase from one of last term's PHSE lessons.

It was very rewarding to see that, for once, her mother was totally lost for words.

7.35 a.m.

Holly Vine's house.
The Cedars, Weston Way, West Green, Dunchester.
Deficit on the H_2O front

Holly Vine slammed the door of the shower cubicle and grabbed her towel. This was all she needed: the weekend from hell, a bad hair day and now this.

'Holly! For the last time, will you hurry up in there?'

her mother yelled from the landing. 'I've got a meeting to go to, remember. What's taking you so long?'

'I'll tell you what's taking so long,' Holly retorted, flinging open the bathroom door and shivering as a blast of cold air hit her legs. 'There's no water.'

'Oh, for pity's sake,' her mother said, turning round and heading for the stairs. 'Don't tell me that wretched boiler has gone out again. Why does it always happen in the middle of winter?'

'No, Mum, you don't get it,' Holly insisted, flicking her nutmeg brown hair out of her eyes, 'I didn't say there was no *hot* water. I said there was no water.'

Angela Vine stopped dead in her tracks. 'No water?' she asked. 'What – you mean, nothing coming out of the taps?'

It's amazing, thought Holly, that a woman who manages to be elected as a local councillor and heads a dozen committees can seem so intensely dim at home.

'Nothing,' Holly repeated as patiently as she could. 'Unless you count a trickle of dark brown sludge as water. I had just started to wash my hair when it stopped all of a sudden.' She glared at her mother. 'And now I've got shampoo in my hair and nothing to rinse it with.'

Her mother punched her fist on the oak banister. 'That does it, then! I have had enough! Roooo-pert! Rupert, get up here now!'

'Mum, cool it,' Holly muttered hastily. 'You know what the doctor said.'

Ever since her dad's heart attack back in the autumn,

she had felt panic-stricken whenever he seemed stressed or moved at more than a snail's pace. Having a dad who was so much older than all her friends' parents was a responsibility – she even tried not to disagree with him. However, that was something of a challenge when faced with a sixty-one-year-old who thought his daughter could exist on ten pounds a week, and who preferred dressing up as a Roundhead and running a tiny Civil War museum in the middle of a field to behaving in an appropriate manner for a retired university lecturer who had just acquired a Senior Citizen's Railcard.

'The doctor,' her mother hissed back at her, 'doesn't live here. If your father chooses to live in a crumbling ruin, he will have to take the consequences. Rupert! Roo-pert!'

'Angela, do you have to yell?' Holly's father asked, coming to the foot of the stairs and almost tripping over Naseby, his Lilac Burmese cat, who made a habit of sitting on people's feet.

'Yes, I do,' his wife replied. 'I've got to be out of the house in half an hour and now Holly says there's no water. Not a drop.'

'Ah,' he muttered.

'Is that all you can say?' his wife retorted. 'Nothing in this house works. The boiler's on its last legs, I've been awake half the night because the windows keep rattling – why we can't get double glazing, heaven knows . . .'

'It would spoil the character of the house, dear,' he

told her mildly. 'The Victorians didn't have replacement windows . . .'

'The Victorians,' Holly butted in, clutching the towel round her and hopping from one foot to the other in an attempt to get warm, 'did, however, have water. We haven't. Why?'

'Ah yes, the water,' mused her dad. 'Now that rings a bell . . .' He tapped the side of his balding head.

Holly sighed. Geriatric parents were a nightmare. It was OK for her brothers – they'd left home ages ago and only came back with their wives and offspring for the odd roast dinner. She, as the afterthought of the family, had to put up with galloping senility every day of her life.

'I remember!' her father exclaimed triumphantly. 'There was a note from Anglian Water. Something about the water being turned off from seven-thirty this morning.'

'You *knew*?' Holly and her mother gasped in unison.

'Didn't I mention it? I felt sure I told you.'

'If you had told me, Dad,' Holly exploded, close to tears, 'I wouldn't be standing here in this state, would I? So when is it coming back on?'

'I think they said around five p.m. tonight,' he ventured.

'Five o'clock?' gasped Holly. 'But I've got to get to school and . . .'

'Rather fun, really, isn't it?' her father cut in. 'Like those TV programmes when people have to live like the Edwardians for a month and . . .'

'I have been living like a flaming Edwardian since the day I married you!' Mrs Vine stormed. 'Rupert, we have to move house. No more excuses. It has to be done.'

Holly didn't know why her mother wasted her breath. Every week for the past six months, she had produced estate agents' details about new houses – and every week her dad had waved his hand dismissively and repeated that the only way he was leaving The Cedars would be feet first in a box.

'Angela, be reasonable,' he replied now, running his fingers through his thinning hair. 'Just because the water authority decide to do some essential work on the sewers, we can hardly uproot and move!'

'Oh, it's not just that – it's everything else, too!' his wife said, sighing. 'The guttering needs replacing, the brickwork needs repointing, the kitchen wouldn't look out of place in your wretched museum . . .'

'And if we sell up, we will be expected to spend shed loads of money tarting the place up,' Holly's father declared. 'It's fine as it is, and besides . . .'

'Never mind all that,' Holly cut in. 'What about my hair?'

'There's some bottled water in the cupboard by the fridge,' her mother told her. 'Use that. And be quick about it.'

Holly took one step towards the stairs.

'Oh, and have you finished that homework? If things don't improve after that dire report card last term . . .'

Holly didn't stop to hear the rest. She'd spent the whole weekend grappling with science and maths and was no nearer to understanding a word of either of them than she had been on Friday night. Her mum didn't seem to understand that Holly couldn't do it any more. Year Ten was too tough; she had chosen all the wrong options back in the summer, just because her parents kept telling her to aim high. As far as Holly could see it, all that happened when you aimed high, was that you fell flat on your face in the mud.

Well, all that was going to change, she thought, stomping down the stairs. Her parents would have to realise that she wasn't put on earth to live out their academic fantasies. Life was too short to worry yourself sick about combustion reactions and integers. She would lay it on the line, tell them how it was . . .

'This decaying monstrosity of a house . . . last week the boiler . . . now no water . . . the roof will fall in next . . . Rupert, are you listening to a word I'm saying?' Her mother's strident tones echoed past.

Then again, Holly thought, perhaps now was not the best time to suggest dropping a whole load of subjects and opting for the easy life.

7.40 a.m.

Tansy Meadows' house, 3 Plough Cottages, Cattle Hill, West Green, Dunchester. The Blues Mother

Tansy Meadows opened her bedroom door and listened. Not a sound.

No discordant singing, no clattering of dishes from the kitchen, no radio blaring out from the sitting room.

It could only mean one thing. Her mum was having a bad day. Again.

Tansy sighed as she stuffed her coursework folders into her school bag. Usually, her mother, who had a track record of choosing the most dire men in the universe to hang out with, bounced back from each broken love affair and within a couple of weeks was her normal embarrassing, madcap self. But not this time.

For the past few weeks, she had either been bursting into tears every few hours or else sitting staring into space and sighing a lot. Even her work as a landscape gardener didn't seem to make her happy any more and Christmas would have been totally dire if it hadn't been for Gran and Mum's sister, Beth, dragging them both up to Scotland for a week. Tansy had missed Andy, her boyfriend, like crazy, but even walks by the loch in the driving rain were preferable to mopping up her mother on an hourly basis. It simply wasn't on: mothers were meant to mop up their kids, not the other way round.

'I guess,' Tansy's friend Holly had said on the phone

the evening before, when Tansy had confessed to being worried about her mother, 'that finding out that the love of your life was planning to con you out of your life savings must leave emotional scars. We did betrayal in psychology last term – it's ever so damaging.'

'Not half as damaging as marrying the hideous Henry would have been,' Tansy retorted. 'Why can't my mum just be glad she had a lucky escape instead of mooning around the place all the time? Some days she doesn't even go to work.'

'Don't worry,' Holly had replied brightly. 'She'll find someone else – she always does.'

'With her track record,' Tansy had said, 'that thought doesn't comfort me at all.'

She hadn't said what she was really thinking, of course. She hadn't said that even though she was fifteen and even though her mum had told her months ago to stop fantasising and accept the truth, she still dreamed that her real dad would turn up and fall madly in love with Mum all over again. He must have loved her all those years ago, when they met at Glastonbury and spent a whole summer together; perhaps he loved her still.

Of course, such ideas were a total waste of time. Her mum had told her that, when she had found out she was pregnant with Tansy, who was named after the fields where her mum had camped that summer, she had written to Pongo five times and even sent a picture of Tansy lying in her Moses basket. And he had never replied.

But of course, she thought, picking up the only photo she had of the dad she had never seen, and running her finger lightly over his smiling face, he was only twenty-two then and probably scared. For all she knew, he could have spent his whole life regretting what he did, or lying awake at nights, dreaming about finding her. Maybe he wondered whether she had inherited his sandy coloured hair, which she had, and tall figure, which sadly she hadn't.

Perhaps . . .

'Tansy! Get down these stairs this minute!' Her mother's shout was loud enough to drown out any thoughts of fathers.

'Won't be a minute,' Tansy began, scrabbling in her drawer for her lip gloss.

'No you won't – because you'll be here in thirty seconds, or else!'

Tansy winced.

'I mean it!'

'OK, OK,' Tansy called, clattering down the uncarpeted stairs and ducking to dodge the Chinese lantern hanging from one of the beams. 'Keep your hair on.'

'Don't you speak to me like that!' her mum stormed, tugging her Betty Boop nightshirt over her ample hips. 'In fact, don't speak to me at all. Look at this!'

She grabbed Tansy by the arm and shoved her through the tiny sitting room and into the cluttered kitchen.

'Just what do you think that is?' her mum demanded, jabbing a finger at the blue plastic washing basket sitting on the draining board.

Tansy looked. Everything was a lurid shade of pink.

'Well?' demanded her mother, running her fingers through her unruly auburn curls. 'Well?'

'You told me not to speak,' Tansy said with grin, hoping against hope that her mother would retrieve her sense of humour.

'Don't push your luck, Tansy Meadows! Did you or did you not put the washing on last night?'

'No,' said Tansy.

'Precisely!' ranted her mum. 'And you shoved your pink sweatshirt in with all my white . . . what do you mean, no?'

'I didn't put it on,' repeated Tansy. 'I offered to, cos I wanted to wash my sweatshirt and you said you'd sort it all later and you would rather I did the dishes.' She glared at her mum. 'So not only did I get to do loads of washing up but now you're accusing me of messing up your laundry. Thanks a bunch!' She whirled round, ready to make a dramatic exit and fend off the next tirade from her mother.

But her mum said nothing. She just sank down into the nearest chair and beg and to sob.

'I'msorryonlyeverythingsgoingwrongand . . .'

'Mum, don't! It's OK!'

Tansy ran up to her and put an arm round her

shaking shoulders. 'It's only clothes,' she stressed, secretly thankful that none of the white stuff was hers. 'You can get some more and . . .'

'Oh sure, and what'll I use for money?' her mum said, weeping. 'It doesn't grow . . .'

'On trees,' finished Tansy. 'I know, you told me.'

'I don't know what's happening to me,' her mum sobbed. 'It's like I haven't got a brain any more . . .'

'Like you ever had one?' Tansy teased.

Her mother gave her a watery smile. 'I'm sorry about yelling.' She sighed, squeezing Tansy's hand. 'It's just that . . .'

. . . *My life's a mess, I feel so lonely, it's OK for you, you've got your life ahead of you*, mouthed Tansy behind her mum's back.

'My life's a mess, I feel so lonely, it's OK for you . . .'

'Mum, stop!' she ordered, trying to quell the rising panic. 'It's all going to work out fine, you'll see. Now go and get dressed, and I'll make toast. Hurry, or you'll be late for work.'

'I'm not going to work.'

'Now that's just plain crazy,' Tansy retorted. 'What would you say to me if I announced I wasn't going to school?'

Honestly, she thought to herself, who is the mother here?

'I can't face it,' her mum cried, tears trickling down her face. 'Some days I feel like I'm going mad.'

'Please, Mum,' Tansy pleaded. 'If you love me one little bit, just try to get a grip. You've said yourself we need the money.'

Her mother sniffed and said nothing.

'And besides, you promised Holly's mum you would clean up her garden . . .'

'She was only taking pity on me. It's January – there's hardly a thing to do. And besides, they're not exactly rolling in money themselves these days. I don't want charity.'

Tansy counted to ten and tried one last time. 'You need to get out of the house,' she insisted. 'How can I concentrate on my school work if I'm worrying about you? Do you want me messing up my grades – you said Year Ten was vital and . . .'

'That,' replied her mother with a faint smile, 'is emotional blackmail.'

'True,' agreed Tansy. 'I learned it from you. Now will you please go upstairs and get dressed. That nightshirt has a hole in a very unsuitable place.'

7.45 a.m.

Jade's house. Politics over the porridge

'Oh, there you are, Jade darling,' her aunt exclaimed as Jade walked into the kitchen. 'We were just talking about you.' She dumped a bowl of porridge in front of Jade and passed her the syrup.

'Why? What have I done?' Jade asked, nibbling on a

broken fingernail. She was all too familiar with Allegra's trick of dropping her in it whenever she felt like it.

'Nothing, silly,' her aunt said, laughing. 'We were just wondering what sort of party you'd like to have on Saturday.'

'She's worried about it costing too much,' Allegra butted in, 'what with you having done up the attic for her and everything.'

How was it that Allegra could invent stories off the top of her head and make them sound believable?

'Can I come to the party?' demanded Helen. 'Can I bring a boy?'

'Helen, you are eight years old and eight-year-olds do not go about with boys,' her mother cut in.

'I do,' replied Helen. 'I'm very soffyhisticated for my age.'

'I mean,' Allegra cut in over everyone's laughter, 'it's only fair, isn't it? Jade didn't get a party last year because of her parents dying, and you said we had to treat her like one of us and I had a disco when I was fifteen.'

'Quite right,' Jade's uncle replied approvingly. 'I think that would be OK, don't you, Paula? Mind you, nothing too pricey . . .'

His wife took a deep breath and forced a bright smile. 'Of course,' she agreed. 'We'll talk about it tonight when you get home from your first aid course, OK?'

Jade wanted to protest, but the lump in her throat made speech impossible.

All she really wanted for her birthday was to be able

to turn the clock back and have her mum and dad alive and well.

And all the parties in the world weren't going to do that.

7.50 a.m.

In the kitchen of The Cedars. Hair-strionics

'Dad, pass me another bottle of water,' Holly mumbled, her head hanging over the kitchen sink. 'And can you take the top off for me? I've got shampoo in my eyes.'

Her father grunted and shoved a bottle into her outstretched hand. 'I know your mother's upset,' he murmured, 'but you don't think she really wants to move house, do you?'

'About as much as she wants to keep breathing,' Holly retorted, pouring the contents of the bottle over her nutmeg brown hair. 'It's not like she hasn't talked about it for . . . DAD!'

She gasped and threw back her head, dripping water all over the floor. 'This isn't water – it's lemonade!' She put her hands to her soaking hair and pulled a face. 'It's all sticky and smelly and . . . Dad, how could you be so stupid?'

'Don't you speak to your father like that,' her mother ordered, bursting into the kitchen with a copy of *Yellow Pages* in her hand. 'Rupert, give her the bottled water.'

'That was the last bottle,' he said.

'How am I supposed to go out like this?' sobbed Holly. 'I'll be a total laughing stock.'

'Oh stop being so dramatic, Holly,' her mother retaliated. 'Blow it dry – it'll be fine. Besides, you're not parading on the catwalk; you're going to school.'

'You have no idea, do you?' retorted Holly. 'Neither of you has the faintest idea about life in the real world.'

8.15 a.m.
Miracles do happen

'You look,' Holly told her reflection in the dressing table mirror, 'like a very bad cartoon.'

She switched her hair-dryer off and tugged at a strand of brown hair at right angles to her left ear.

'Holly, it's eight-fifteen!' her mother called up the stairs. 'If you want a lift, I'm leaving now! Otherwise you'll have to walk.'

She grabbed her bag and ran down the stairs.

'You left your phone on the worktop,' her mother said, tossing it to her as she opened the front door. 'It rang.'

'So why didn't you call me?' demanded Holly. 'It might have been urgent.'

'Not half as urgent as getting you out of the front door,' she replied grimly. 'Get in the car.'

Holly ambled across the gravel drive, flipping open the cover of her phone.

'VOICEMAIL MESSAGE'

She punched the call button.

'Hi there. It's Kyle.'

Holly gasped. 'Oh my God, oh my God, oh my God!' It had happened. He'd called.

'What on earth's the matter?' her mother demanded, slamming the car door and turning the ignition key.

'What? Sssh, I'm listening.' She pressed the phone to her right ear and stuck her finger in the left one. 'Mum, drive quietly,' she insisted, as her mother revved the engine.

'Remember me?'

Remember you? Holly thought. How could any girl in her right mind ever forget you?

'We met at Tansy's mother's wedding – well, not quite wedding.'

Holly's mind flashed back to the day Tansy's mum was due to marry this guy called Henry. It was Kyle, whose mum had been conned out of loads of cash by the wretched man, who had turned up and denounced Tansy's future stepfather as a cheat and a liar.

'Anyway, I've been wanting to call you for ages but so much has happened and . . . need to talk to you . . . but I . . . when . . . because . . .'

'Oh, no, it's breaking up!' gasped Holly.

' . . . so if . . . could meet . . .'

The line went dead.

'I don't believe it!' Holly shook her phone in fury. 'I wait weeks for a call and then he loses the signal!'

'He?' Her mother turned to look at her and narrowly missed the gatepost at the end of their drive. 'What do you mean, he? Who?'

'Hey, look – what's going on over there?' said Holly.

She pointed across the road to where a couple of workmen were unloading gear from a large white van and dumping it in the front garden of The Laurels, the old house that had been empty and up for sale for weeks. Not, of course, that she had the slightest interest in what was happening; but since she had no intention of telling her mother anything about her private life, particularly the bit involving a seventeen-year-old boy, it seemed as good a distraction as any.

And it worked. Her mother stamped on the brake.

'Oh, Holly!' she gasped. 'They've sold it! And look . . . oh, that's wonderful! Now I can get things sorted!'

'Excuse me?' Holly queried wondering if her mother was once again losing the plot. Her mother zapped the window down and peered out. 'Acquired for Apple Tree Nurseries,' she read from the large board being hammered into the front garden. 'We're home and dry, Holly darling, home and dry!'

Holly opened her mouth to ask her mother what on earth she was on about, and then decided against it.

The chances of the answer making any sense at all were very remote indeed.

8.20 a.m.
Baby talk

Tansy stood shivering on Andy's doorstep, her finger pressing the bell for the third time.

'For the last time, will someone get that?' She heard her boyfriend's father's voice booming from the back of the house, rapidly followed by the high-pitched shrieking of a baby.

'Allan, for pity's sake, you've woken Clover now!'

There was a rattling of a door chain, and the door burst open. Andy's mum stood in the doorway in her bathrobe, one red faced baby on her left hip and another drooling over her right shoulder.

'Oh, Tansy dear, it's you!' she gasped. 'Come in. Andy! It's Tansy!'

The drooling baby puckered its face, took a deep breath and began yelling in unison with its sister.

'Take Baz for me, there's an angel,' Andy's mother said, thrusting the infant into Tansy's arms. 'He'll quieten down in a minute. I'll go and hurry Andy along.'

'Baz?' queried Tansy. 'I thought you had called him Ginger.'

'The family didn't approve,' sighed Mrs Richards, patting the baby on the head. 'So it's Basil. Goes well with Clover, doesn't it? I like plant names.'

It is, thought Tansy, comforting to know that I'm not the only one round here with a totally insane mother.

Baz took one look at Tansy and screamed twice as loudly, his little face turning an alarming shade of puce.

'I don't know what to do,' Tansy began, but Mrs Richards was already half way up the stairs, Clover bouncing on her hip.

'There, there,' Tansy murmured nervously at the wailing baby. 'Hush.'

She patted his back. To her surprise, Baz stopped yelling and stared at her.

'Good baby,' Tansy cooed.

Baz hiccupped and threw up down her jacket.

'Oh, my God!' she gasped, wrinkling her nose in disgust and holding Baz at arm's length. 'Mrs Richards! Help!'

She looked round wildly for somewhere to put the baby. Just then, Andy, came crashing down the stairs, yawning loudly, his shirt hanging out and glasses skewed on his nose, .

'Hi, gorgeous!' He smiled wearily, coming towards her, lips already puckered.

'Keep away from me!' she shouted, backing off.

'Oh great – I haven't seen you in three days and – '

'It's not you – it's the baby! He's been sick all down me. Can you take him?'

'Are you mad?' Andy asked, recoiling. 'That one could puke for England. God, I hate babies!'

'Andy, you know you adore them both.'

His mother came clattering down the stairs, a nappy bag in one hand and paused to sniff the air. 'Oh dear – has he been sick?'

'Yes,' Tansy said, thrusting the baby at Mrs Richards, and unzipping her jacket. 'All over me.'

'Oh no, I'm so sorry,' Mrs Richards murmured.

'Can you shove this in your washing machine?' Tansy asked, emptying her pockets and dropping her mobile phone into her school bag. 'No way can I turn up at school stinking like this.'

'Of course,' she replied, taking the baby and planting a kiss on the top of its head. 'Is Bazzy Wazzy feeling sicky wicky, den?'

Andy raised his eyebrows. 'Not half as sicky wicky as all that baby talk makes me!' he retorted. 'Come on, Tansy, let's go.'

'You can't go out like that,' Mrs Richards said, grabbing Tansy's arm. 'You'll freeze to death. Borrow my anorak.' She gestured to a shapeless sludge-coloured garment hanging on a hook by the front door.

I would rather die of hypothermia, Tansy thought.

'I'll be fine,' she said, smiling sweetly, trying to ignore the rancid odour emanating from her own jacket lying on the floor at her feet. 'This sweatshirt's very warm.'

'I insist,' Andy's mum said firmly, thrusting it into her hands and opening the front door. 'What would your mother say if she thought you were walking the streets in January without a coat?'

What was it, Tansy thought, about parents and coats? She'll be offering me a vest next.

'Come to think of it,' Andy's mum mused. 'I've got some thermal undies upstairs, left over from skiing and . . .'

'The jacket's fine,' Tansy mumbled, grabbing the hideous garment. 'Come on, Andy – we'll be late.'

'Put it on, now,' Mrs Richards ordered. 'There, isn't that better?'

Better than what? Tansy thought, catching sight of her reflection in the hall mirror. Death by drowning?

8.30 a.m.
Big brother speak

'Are you OK?' Tansy asked Andy, pulling off the hideous jacket and rolling it into the smallest possible ball.

'Oh sure,' replied Andy sarcastically. 'I've been awake half the night thanks to screeching babies and a brother who talks in his sleep, Dad's in a foul temper all the time and Mum . . .'

'Exhausted and grumpy?' Tansy asked.

'No, that's what's so odd,' Andy muttered. 'Two totally unplanned babies, and it's like she's on a permanent high. Sings off-key all the time, doesn't seem to notice the total tip that the house has become and slops around in her bathrobe uttering infant-speak.' He sighed. 'I guess that is what's winding Dad up,' he added.

Tansy didn't know what to say. Ever since Andy's mum had disappeared for six months and returned home pregnant, no one, not even the parents, had mentioned the subject. She couldn't help wondering whether those little babies would end up like her – never knowing who their real dad was. And whether they would ever give up trying to find him.

Andy yawned.

'I don't suppose,' he said tentatively, 'that your mum would let me sleep at your house for a couple of nights? Just to be in a sane and peaceful atmosphere would be so cool.'

Tansy pulled a face and snapped her thoughts back to the present.

'I'll ask her,' she grinned. 'But if it's sanity you're looking for, you're looking in the wrong place.'

8.50 a.m.

In the locker room at West Green College

'Tansy, I've been looking for you everywhere,' Holly cried. 'You said you'd wait at the gate.' She peered at her friend who was hugging the radiator in the locker room. 'You will never guess who has just phoned me,' Holly said, clapping her fists together in excitement.

'By the look of you, someone male, someone you fancy, someone you'd given up hope of ever seeing again. Which means Kyle, right?'

'Yes!' Holly punched the air and hugged Tansy.

'Cool. So what did he want?' Tansy asked, hitching her bag over her shoulder.

'We got cut off,' Holly admitted, pulling her mobile from her pocket. 'But he did say he'd been wanting to call for ages. And something about meeting up!'

She hugged herself and jiggled from one foot to the other. 'I'm going to call him right now,' she breathed. 'Can you keep a lookout for old Grubb? You know what he's like about phones in school.'

Holly dialled Kyle's mobile.

'The number you have dialled has not been recognised. Please check and try . . .'

'What? It must be recognised – he rang me, you stupid woman!'

Tansy nudged Holly's elbow. 'Hurry,' she urged her. 'The second bell's just gone and Old Grubb will be on the rampage any minute now.'

Holly ignored her and punched the phone again. 'This woman said it was a wrong number,' she said. 'And she's doing it again! Listen, woman . . .'

'Holly, it's a recording,' Tansy said patiently. 'There is no woman there. Hey, quick . . .'

'I know that!' Holly cut in. 'I can't believe this is happening.'

'And what precisely can't you believe, Holly Vine?' Mr Grubb, the form tutor, came up behind her, hand held out. 'Your phone, if you please.'

Holly gasped and stared up at him pleadingly.

'I tried to warn you,' whispered Tansy.

'I'm sorry, Sir – it's my mother,' Holly improvised

hastily. 'She's not well – I was just phoning . . .'

'Dear me, not well?'

'No, Sir – really poorly, actually.'

'So poorly,' replied Mr Grubb dryly, 'that she gave me a cheery wave as she drove off from the school gates not ten minutes ago? You may collect your phone at the end of the day.'

'But, Sir . . .'

'And if you argue, I shall keep it all week,' he replied. 'Now get to class and try to concentrate on the important things in life.'

Holly glared at his retreating back. 'Like he'd really know what they were,' she muttered.

8.55 a.m.
On the way to registration

'Hi, Scott,' Tansy said, thumping him on the back. 'How was America? Lucky you, missing the first week of term.'

'The head's not too chuffed about it, but it was sure worth it!' Scott grinned. 'Have you seen Jade?'

8.57 a.m.

'Hi Scott,' Cleo said, sidling up to him. 'How was America?'

'Cool,' he replied. 'Have you seen . . .'

'And Trig?' she gabbled. 'How was Trig?'

'OK,' he said. 'Have you seen Jade?'

OK? What did OK mean? Cleo thought, nibbling at a

hang nail. OK wasn't as good as 'Good' or 'Cool' or 'Fine'.

Perhaps he'd split with the new girlfriend. Perhaps seeing Trig had reawakened memories of being with Cleo and he was wishing he'd never dumped her.

Get real, she told herself with a sigh. Scott is a guy. 'OK' was probably the full extent of his vocabulary. It probably meant nothing at all.

9.00 a.m.

Crisis of confidence

'Listen,' Cleo said the moment Holly reached her table. 'You're my friend, right?'

'Course I am,' said Holly, dropping her voice as Mr Grubb called for silence and began taking the register.

'So – you'd say it like it is, right?'

'Say what like what is?' whispered Holly.

'I'm a mess, aren't I?' Cleo mumbled, scuffing the toe of her boot against the table leg.

'What do you mean?'

'I'm a blob, a spotty, fat . . .'

'Cleo, you're not fat,' Holly cut in, raising her voice in an attempt to console her friend. 'I would kill to have a chest like yours. Come to think of it, I'd kill to have any chest at all.'

'And I talk funny, right?' Cleo went on.

Holly sighed and shook her head. 'Cleo, what are you on about? You talk like everyone else round here.'

'And you, Miss Vine, talk far too much!' Mr Grubb loomed over her, register in hand. 'First the phone, now your incessant chattering. This is not a good start to the week.'

'No, Sir. Sorry, Sir.'

Holly waited until the form tutor had retreated to the other side of the room.

'What's brought all this on?' she mouthed to Cleo.

'My mother,' began Cleo. 'She says . . .'

'Stop right there,' interjected Holly. 'And stop worrying. Just remember that ninety per cent of what mothers say is total rubbish.'

10.45 a.m.

In English

'Do you think if I play it all humble and meek, old Grubb will give me back my phone at lunchtime?' Holly whispered to Tansy.

'No chance,' said Tansy. 'He gets his kicks from being difficult.'

'What if I try to call Kyle from the payphone?' mouthed Holly.

'It was a wrong number, remember?' muttered Tansy from behind her hand. 'It's not going to turn into a right one just because you use a different phone.'

'Oh my God, that's it! Don't you see?' Holly said. 'He must have changed his mobile number. The one I've got must be out of date.'

'Right,' murmured Tansy.

'So as soon as I get my phone back, I'm going to check the number he called me from and ring that,' Holly declared. 'Neat, eh?'

'Amazing,' said Tansy, sighing.

11.10 a.m.

In Tansy Meadows' kitchen. Straight talking between parents

While Tansy was handing out advice in the school playground, her mother was getting a whole basinful of it in the kitchen of their cottage.

'Clarity, what on earth's going on?' Holly's mum demanded, having burst through the unlocked back door. 'I got back from my meeting – honestly, I sometimes think I'm a lone voice in the wilderness on these committees – and you weren't there.'

'Where?' Tansy's mother asked, cradling a mug of coffee in her hands.

'You were meant to be coming over today to give me advice on making the wretched garden easier to manage, remember?'

'Oh, yes. Sorry.'

'I mean, it's OK – I know you're busy but I was worried that something might have happened,' Holly's mum replied anxiously.

'I've got a cold,' Tansy's mother said hastily, hoping

to explain away both her red-rimmed eyes and the fact that she was still in her nightshirt and ancient fleece.

'No, you haven't,' replied Holly's mum calmly. 'You've been crying. Henry, is it?'

'Why does everyone think it has to be about Henry? I'm fine about Henry; I'm over Henry, as far as I'm concerned Henry can go hang . . .'

'So, it's about Henry,' nodded Holly's mum. 'Can I make myself a coffee? It's icy out there.'

'Sure.'

'So come on,' Mrs Vine insisted, picking up the kettle and filling it at the sink. 'Tell Auntie Angie.'

Tansy's mother sighed. 'It's not that I want him back,' she said, sniffing, getting to her feet and spooning coffee into a mug. 'He's a swine, I know that. It's just . . .'

'It's just that you feel so let down, you feel all alone, you feel some days as if anyone would be better than no one at all. Am I right?'

'How did you know?'

'Holly's trained me very well. Thing is, she's fifteen and you're thirty-five . . .'

'Thirty-two,' Tansy's mother corrected her hastily.

'That young? God, I can't even remember thirty-two. Come to think of it, remembering fifty-two is a struggle.' She sighed. 'Anyway, you've got plenty of time to meet the right person. But you won't do it moping around here, looking like a rag bag . . .'

'Oh, thanks.'

'You're welcome,' said Holly's mother with a smile. 'That's what friends are for. So – when we've had the coffee, you're going to get dressed and come over to my place. We have things to do.'

'But the ground's frozen solid . . .'

'Who said anything about gardening?' Holly's mother grinned. 'I thought more along the lines of cream cakes and a glass of something sparkly. I won the raffle at the WI. By the way, did you know you had a hole in that nightshirt?'

1.00 p.m.
Image consultation

'It's not like I want to go on the wretched show,' Cleo concluded, having told Holly the whole saga of *Like Mother, Like Daughter*. 'It's just all that stuff Mum said made me realise that I look just the same now as I did a year ago – dumpy, dull . . .'

'Stop right there!' demanded Holly, edging forward to the sandwich cabinet and peering inside. 'You want to change your image, right? So change it!'

'Oh sure – like, how?'

'I don't know,' retorted Holly impatiently, grabbing a tuna mayonnaise wrap, 'Get highlights in your hair, dye your eyelashes, use fake tan, get new clothes.' She reeled off all the articles she could remember from the previous week's copy of *Flourish!* magazine.

'I can't afford all that!' Cleo protested, picking up a plate of cannelloni and sniffing it. 'Roy's cut my allowance.'

'So do the makeover stuff at home, then,' shrugged Holly. 'You can get kits . . .'

'Holly, *would* you? Really? That would be so amazing!'

'Would I what?' Holly queried.

'Do it for me,' Cleo gabbled. 'The hair especially?'

'I don't know . . .'

'Only you're so stylish,' Cleo coaxed.

'Am I? Do you honestly think so?'

Holly peered at her reflection in the Perspex top of the chilled snacks cabinet.

'OK, then. I'll do it. But on one condition.'

Cleo frowned. 'What's that?'

'You move on,' ordered Holly. 'No more mooning over Trig.'

Cleo sighed. 'I guess,' she said. 'OK, it's a deal. From now on, the name of Trig won't pass my lips.'

1.10 p.m.

In the school cafeteria. Pasta and pretence

'Hi, Scott!' Jade murmured, wincing slightly from Allegra's constant prodding in the small of her back. 'Mind if I sit here?' She gestured to the free seat at his side.

'It's a free country,' Scott muttered.

'Scott's got these amazing photos,' Holly said. 'They had a white Christmas, the lucky things – look!' She shoved a couple of photos under Jade's nose.

Surely Holly and Scott aren't getting it together again after all this time? thought Jade, noticing the scowl on Allegra's face. That could complicate matters big time.

'Say something,' Allegra hissed in Jade's left ear.

'You look . . . cold,' Jade stammered.

'It was ten below,' Scott said proudly. 'Look, here's one of me and Trig skating . . .'

'Let's see!' Cleo lunged across the table and grabbed the top picture.

'Cleo, what did I say?' muttered Holly in singsong tones.

Cleo sighed and shoved the picture back across the table. 'You and who skating?' she asked.

'Have we missed anything?' Tansy asked, as she and Andy pushed their way through to the table, ripping the wrappers off tuna wraps with their teeth.

'Jade's having a party,' Scott said with a grin. 'Saturday. And we're going to . . .'

'Wow, is that the Chicago Bears?' Andy put his hand on Tansy's shoulder and leaned across the table, prodding the pile of photos beside Scott. 'I've seen them on Sky Sports. Scott, don't tell me you got to go to a game?'

'Yeah,' nodded Scott, who appeared to have cultivated a Midwest twang. 'And we got VIP seats because of Trig's uncle – that's him there.' He stabbed his finger at another picture. 'He is some high-powered businessman and gets all these freebies.'

'You lucky thing,' Andy cried, glancing at the photo and tossing it to one side.

'I know – it was just the finest game – they scored in the first . . .'

'Here we go,' Holly sighed, raising her eyebrows at Tansy. 'Sports talk. I'm off.'

'Me, too.' Jade nodded, pushing back her chair. 'I'm on library duty. Coming, Tansy?'

Tansy didn't reply. She kept staring at the picture lying on the table in front of her.

'And this one was taken on my last night there,' Scott went on. 'The whole family went to see the fireworks at Navy Pier – it was a blast.'

'Isn't that the same guy?' Tansy broke in, snatching the photo from his hand. 'The one that took you to the match?'

She glanced from one photograph to the other.

Scott nodded. 'Yeah. Like I said, he's Trig's uncle. Why?'

Tansy shook her head. 'Nothing,' she said. 'I was just . . . nothing.'

2.00 p.m.

Not concentrating on human physiology

You're mad, Tansy Meadows, she told herself. It's a total impossibility. As if. Get a grip, girl, for God's sake.

2.05 p.m.
Concentrating even less

OK, so Mum confessed that my dad went back to live in Illinois. Fifteen years ago. Forget it.

2.20 p.m.

I said, forget it.

3.00 p.m.

'It's going to be so cool,' Allegra enthused as she and Jade changed after PE.

'What is?'

'Your party,' stressed Allegra.

Jade sighed. 'I suppose I can't get out of it, now you've opened your big mouth?'

'Not if you value your reputation.' Allegra grinned.

3.30 and one second

'Can I have my phone back now, Sir?' Holly asked, the very instant the end of afternoon bell rang.

Mr Grubb sniffed. 'I suppose so,' he said grudgingly. 'But if I see you using it again in school time . . .'

'I won't, Sir. Thank you, Sir. Bye, Sir.'

'Wait!' Mr Grubb interjected. 'I don't seem to have seen your science homework. Where is it?'

Oh sugar, thought Holly.

'I left it at home, Sir,' she said meekly. 'We got our water cut off . . .'

'And that prevented you from picking up your project, did it?' Mr Grubb said sarcastically. 'Bring it tomorrow or it's detention, you understand?'

But I can't do it, she wanted to scream. I hate science, I don't get what it's all about. I haven't even got to question two yet.

'Yes, Sir,' she mumbled. 'Thank you, Sir.'

3.35 p.m.
Disappointment

Holly dashed to the locker room out of sight of teachers and punched the Received Calls menu.

'Oh no – I don't believe it! Tansy, over here!' She shoved the phone under Tansy's nose.

'UNKNOWN.'

'Now what do I do?' she wailed.

'You can't *do* anything, can you?' Tansy snapped. 'What's the big deal, anyway?'

Holly stared at her. 'Oh, charming!' she muttered. 'Just because your love-life is totally sussed . . .'

'Sorry, I've just got stuff on my mind,' Tansy said with a sigh. 'Got to dash – talk later, OK? And don't worry, he's bound to phone sooner or later.'

I wish, Holly thought to herself, that I could be so sure.

3.40 p.m.
At the school gates

'You don't know where Tansy is, do you?' Andy asked, running to catch up with Holly.

'Gone home,' muttered Holly.

'Terrific,' said Andy. 'There goes another night's sleep.'

'Pardon?'

'I asked if I could sleep at her place tonight,' he explained, 'just to escape yelling babies. She was going to ask her mum.'

'That must have been what was on her mind,' Holly assured him. 'She'll have dashed off to bribe her mother. Two cups of tea and a quick scoot round with the vacuum usually does it.'

4.15 p.m.
Tansy's house. Wondering

Tansy sat on the bed, staring at the photograph in its silver frame.

The hair's a bit different in the other photo, she thought. *But then it would be, fifteen years on, wouldn't it? But the heart-shaped face, the big nose, and the sticking-out ears – they are all the same.*

She peered closely at the picture. When her mum had given it to her, it had been torn in a couple of places and she'd mended it with Sellotape. The Sellotape neatly covered up the scar on his . . .

The scar! Did the guy in Scott's photo have a scar?

She scanned her memory, trying to conjure up Scott's photos in her head. I have to find out, she thought. Whatever it takes, I have to know.

4.17 p.m.

This is crazy, Tansy thought. The odds of it being him are zillions to one against. I need my head seeing to.

4.19 p.m.

But there's no harm in trying to find out.

4.30 p.m.

'Hi, Jade, it's me, Tansy. Look, I need a favour.'

'If it's that German translation,' Jade shouted down the phone, 'forget it. I can't do it either!'

'It's not,' Tansy assured her. 'You know those photos Scott was showing us?'

'What about them? You'll have to speak up – I'm in Abbey Street and the traffic's mad.'

'Can you get that photo of Scott at the match? Or the one at the fireworks?' Tansy shouted. 'For me to borrow? I thought if you asked for one, it wouldn't look odd, what with you and him . . .'

There was a clattering and scraping noise at the other end of the phone and a muffled scream from Jade.

'For God's sake, what the hell do you think . . .?' Tansy heard her yell.

The irritation in Jade's voice took Tansy by surprise. 'I was only asking,' she began.

There was a clunking sound and the phone went dead.

Charming, thought Tansy. Thanks a million.

4.30 p.m.
Chance encounter

'For God's sake, what the hell do you think you're doing?' Jade gasped, staggering across the pavement as her phone flew out of her hand. She was almost knocked off her feet by a wiry girl in torn jeans belting down the street and slamming into her.

'Ouch!' The girl's booted foot caught Jade's ankle, and Jade stumbled and fell, sprawling across the pavement.

'It wasn't my fault!' The girl was panting, her cheeks flushed and her eyes suspiciously bright. 'I didn't mean . . . it was them, I . . .' She gestured over her shoulder as Jade hauled herself to her feet, and grabbed her phone from a pile of leaves in the gutter. 'They were laying into me so I just ran,' the girl concluded, running her fingers through her spiky bleached hair.

Jade followed her gaze. Three girls were standing on the corner, shouting abuse and making rude gestures. As they caught her eye, they sniggered and ran off.

'It's OK,' Jade replied, rubbing her knee. 'Hey, I know

you. You're Brooke Sylvester. You were new last term. Miss Partridge's tutor group?'

'Yeah,' grunted Brooke.

'Thought so.' Jade nodded. 'Didn't you get suspended for . . .'

'Nose studs,' finished Brooke, rubbing the back of her hand across her face. 'Stupid rule or what?'

'Talking of noses, did you know yours is bleeding?' Jade gasped. 'You must have banged it when you crashed into me.'

Brooke shrugged. 'I get them sometimes,' she muttered, dabbing ineffectually at her left nostril with a none-too-clean finger. 'It's no big deal.'

'You've got to pinch your nose, just here,' Jade informed her, dead chuffed to be able to put her first aid training into practice on something other than an inflatable dummy. 'And breathe through your mouth. Relax, and . . .'

'Get off me!' Brooke snapped, pushing Jade away.

'Sorry,' Jade mumbled, pulling a packet of tissues from her jacket pocket and thrusting them at the girl. 'I was only trying to help.'

'I'm OK,' Brooke muttered. 'It's stopping. Look, I didn't know it was you – I mean, you're not wearing uniform.' She made it sound as if Jade had committed a crime.

'I've been to my first aid class – you know, for the Duke of Edinburgh Award,' she said. 'We're allowed to change into a tracksuit.'

'I wouldn't have – I mean, I'm sorry. Really.'

'Don't worry about it,' Jade said, rubbing her ankle. 'It wasn't your fault those girls had it in for you.'

'Yes, well . . .'

Brooke looked warily up and down the road. It was clear that she was pretty uptight.

'Do you want me to phone someone?' Jade asked. 'Your mum or someone?'

'Oh, sure! Like she'd be a real help.'

Jade swallowed. 'Well, I mean, I'm sure she'd be worried if . . .'

'You don't know the half of it!' retorted Brooke, her face flushing. She eyed Jade up and down. 'I suppose your mum would come running the moment you said "Ouch!", is that it?'

'My mum's dead,' Jade said flatly.

Brooke bit her lip. 'Oh. Sorry. I didn't know.'

'Why should you?' Jade asked. 'Look, if you're scared of bumping into those kids again . . .'

'Do I look scared?' snapped Brooke. 'It's just . . . I haven't got money for my bus fare because they took it off me, and . . .'

'Took it off you? That's awful. Who are they anyway?'

'Just some girls,' said Brooke. 'They live on my estate. That's why I want to get the bus so I can beat them home.'

'I've only got a five-pound note.' Jade hesitated, pulling it from her pocket.

'Nice one!' Brooke whipped it out of Jade's hand as

her face broke into a broad grin that dimpled her cheeks. 'I'll pay you back tomorrow, OK?'

With that, she broke into a run back up the street.

'Hey,' called Jade. 'Take it easy. Your nose . . .'

But Brooke had already turned the corner and was out of sight.

7.00 p.m.

In Tansy's kitchen. In shock

'Mum – you're humming,' Tansy commented in amazement. 'Well, it's either that or you're in pain.'

To her delight, her mother actually laughed. 'I can hum in my own kitchen, can't I? I feel better.'

'So what made the difference?' Tansy asked. 'You haven't gone and met . . .'

'I haven't met anyone, silly. You've got a one-track mind.'

Tansy grinned. 'I wonder which bit of my gene pool that came from,' she murmured.

7.00 p.m.

Sighing over science

I can't do it. I don't get it. It doesn't make sense.

Holly stared at her homework. She felt like crying. What was happening to her? she thought. I used to be able to do school work, no problem. But lately, it was like her brain had turned to jelly. It wasn't her fault, it was the stupid system. You should be allowed to do the things you were good at and drop the rest.

Except that there wasn't much she was good at. Except art and English. And French, on a good day. She'd fail everything else, she just knew she would.

Perhaps food would make her brain work again. She'd be better after supper.

7.10 p.m.

Holly's house. Paternal protests

'How dare they?' Holly's father burst into the kitchen still wearing his outdoor coat and hurled his briefcase on to the table. 'That is positively not on! It's an outrage, it's . . .'

'Rupert!' his wife cried.

'Dad!' Holly burst out at the same moment.

'Calm down!' they both finished.

'Calm down? You obviously haven't seen what's going on over the road,' he exploded. 'The Laurels . . .'

'Is sold.' Holly's mother smiled. 'I know. Sit down, dear, and have a glass of wine. Supper's ready.'

'But have you seen the sign?' he stormed, grabbing the corkscrew from the kitchen drawer. 'Do you know what it says?'

'Sold, perhaps?' suggested Holly, flinging cutlery on to the table.

'It says,' thundered Mr Vine, '*Acquired for Apple Tree Nurseries.*' He yanked the cork from the wine bottle and frowned at his wife, who was calmly dishing cauliflower cheese on to plates. 'Did you know anything about this?'

'Me, dear?' queried Holly's mother. 'I'm not on the Planning Committee.'

'It's about the only ruddy committee you're not on,' he grunted, taking a slurp of wine. 'Still, you're a local councillor – can't you protest?'

'About what, precisely?'

'About this outrage – messing about with a beautiful early Victorian mansion like that and selling it to some tacky garden centre.'

'Oh, Rupert,' she said, sighing.

'Dad, it's a hideous heap,' Holly maintained. 'They should knock it down and . . .' Her thoughts on architectural improvement were interrupted by the vibrating of her phone in her pocket. She grabbed it and flipped open the cover. 'Hi!'

'Holly, not at the table!' snapped her mother.

'*Hi, Holly – got you at last. It's Kyle.*' Holly's heart leapt as she heard the Scottish lilt in his voice.

'Holly!' her mother stormed, leaning across the table and attempting to grab the phone. 'Did you hear what I said?'

Holly gestured to her mother to keep quiet. 'Hi,' she said, trying to sound sexily husky, which was a trifle difficult with a mouthful of piping-hot cauliflower. 'Hang on.' She leapt up from the table and rushed out into the hall.

'Look, I need your help,' Kyle began.

Anything, she thought. Absolutely anything.

'Have you got Tansy Meadows' mobile number?'

Her stomach nearly joined the cauliflower in her mouth. 'Tansy?' Well, perhaps not anything.

'Not sure,' she lied. 'What's it about? Maybe I can help.'

'*Holly!*' Her mother flung open the kitchen door.

Holly waved a hand at her and galloped up the stairs.

'I wouldn't have bothered you, but your number was the only one I could find. You gave it to me after the wedding, remember . . .'

I gave it to you, thought Holly, so that you could phone me and ask me out, not so that you could use me as Directory Enquiries.

'Of course, I guess I could call round at her place,' Kyle went on. 'I think I can remember where it is, but the thing is . . .'

'Call round?' Holly replied. 'But you're miles away.'

Which is the prime reason we never got it together, she added in her head. It was easier to blame the two-hour train journey rather than her lack of personal allure.

'Not any more,' he replied. 'We moved up here just before Christmas because Mum . . . oh well, it's a long story. But that's why I need Tansy's number.'

Holly's mind was racing. Kyle was living in

Dunchester. If she played her cards right . . .

'OK,' she said. 'It's 07975 333224. She might be switched off, though, if she's out with her boyfriend.' She emphasised the last word as heavily as she dared.

'No worries,' Kyle said. 'Holly, you're a star.'

She was about to say something flirtatious and enticing. But he'd hung up.

7.15 p.m.
Giving orders

'Tansy? It's me. No, not Jade, silly. Holly. Now listen . . .' She rattled off the saga of Kyle's phone call. 'I don't know what he wants, but you've got Andy and he'd be devastated if you chucked him and I . . . well, yes of course I want him. You will? And you'll drop my name into the conversation loads of times? Brilliant. Bye!'

7.45 p.m.
Hot wires

'Tansy? It's me. Jade. Sorry we got cut off. What? No, of course I didn't slam the phone down, silly. There was this girl . . .'

Tansy shuffled her bottom into a more comfortable position on the end of her bed as Jade described what had happened.

'Are you sure you're not hurt?' Tansy asked. 'Oh

good. Now about the photos . . . Yes, I get the point. You don't want Scott to think you're keen. But couldn't you just pretend to want one of the photos? As a memento or something?'

She winced as a tirade came back at her down the phone.

'I wouldn't ask you but it's vital,' she said. 'Really. What? Of course I don't fancy him, you dweeb. And no, I can't ask him myself. I don't want him to know about . . .'

She hesitated.

'You won't tell a living soul, if I tell you something? Promise? OK.'

She took a deep breath.

'I think Trig's uncle might be my long lost dad. Now will you get the photo?'

8.15 p.m.
The die is cast

'Wonderful! Thrilling! See you all then! *Ciao!*'

Cleo's mum replaced the handset and spun round like a whirling dervish. 'Yes, *yes*, *yes*!' she cried, clapping her hands. 'We're in!'

'In where, precisely?' Cleo asked.

'The show, darling,' her mother beamed. 'You and me. Of course, we've got to audition in a couple of weeks but that'll be a piece of cake!'

'Mum, I told you I wasn't going to do it,' Cleo

shouted. 'How dare you!'

'You'll love it, darling,' her mother assured her. 'They were thrilled – said they were overrun with in-your-face, trendy teens and all they needed now was a couple of perfectly sensible, ordinary . . . well, I mean . . .'

Did they now? thought Cleo. That's very interesting.

'Anyway, we might not get chosen,' Diana rattled on. 'What is there to lose?'

Between now and then? Around half a stone, five zits and a clutch of broken fingernails, thought Cleo.

'My principles,' she said. Not to mention my oh-so-boring image.

8.30 p.m.

Jade's house. Round table negotiations

'Right, about this party,' Jade's aunt began, as she dished out portions of apple charlotte. 'You can have fifteen friends . . .'

'Twenty,' Allegra interrupted. 'Unfair to leave anyone special out.'

'No alcohol, of course. Seven-thirty till ten-thirty . . .'

'Ten-thirty?' Allegra butted in. 'We're not kindergarten kids. Midnight?'

'Eleven,' said her mother.

'Honestly, I don't mind . . .' Jade muttered.

'Eleven-thirty,' pushed Allegra. 'And you and Dad go out.'

'Absolutely not!' Paula cried.

'I'd like a night out,' her husband commented, pouring the remains of the custard over his dessert. 'And Helen will be at that friend's sleepover. We can ask Josh to be in charge.'

Jade and Allegra eyed one another. Josh was almost eighteen but he couldn't take care of his collection of stick insects without losing half a dozen under the fridge.

'Josh might be working at the pub that night,' his wife reminded him. 'We can't go and leave the girls.'

'Nonsense,' her husband said. 'You can't mollycoddle them for ever. We'll leave phone numbers and choose a restaurant nearby . . .'

'Great!' cried Allegra. 'That's settled then. Now, who do we – I mean, who are you going to invite, Jade?'

9.45 p.m.

The Cedars. Grappling with combustion reactions

I still can't do it. I don't care. Let him give me detention, silly old . . . Anyway, if it's that bad, maybe he'll tell me to drop it and do easier stuff. Who needs GCSE science anyway? I'm going to wash my hair. Again.

9.47 p.m.

'Mum!' Holly shrieked down the stairs. 'There's no hot water!'

'Good, absolutely splendid!' her mother yelled back.

I am, sighed Holly to herself, surrounded by idiots.

10.00 p.m.

In Jade's bedroom. Being manipulated

'Let's remind ourselves who's coming. Me and you, Scott of course, Tansy and Andy, Holly and Cleo, Ursula, Alex, Tim, Polly, Iain, Becky and Warren – hey, you could have Warren; he's single right now . . .'

'Allegra, shut up and go to bed,' pleaded Jade. 'Galloping acne would be preferable to Warren Hudson. And whose party is it, anyway?'

'Yours,' said Allegra. 'But since you said you didn't really want one, I thought I'd take over, OK? Night!

10.10 p.m.

Cleo's house. Motherly persuasion

'If you'll do it, darling,' said Mrs Greenway, 'you can have a quarter of the fee.'

'Which would come to how much exactly?'

'Two hundred and fifty pounds,' her mum said, and smiled.

Two hundred and fifty pounds! Now you're talking.

'And I get that even if we don't get further than the first round?' queried Cleo.

'Yes,' said her mother.

'Will you put that in writing?'

'If you want me to,' her mother sighed.

'Done!' said Cleo.

10.05 p.m.

3 Plough Cottages. In bed

Please God, let it be him, whispered Tansy, taking one last look at the photograph by her bed. And if it is him, let me know what to do. And make him move to England and fall in love with Mum all over again. Amen.

TUESDAY

8.30 a.m.

West Green College. Biting the bullet

'Hey, Scott, wait!' Jade called, running after him across the schoolyard. 'Look, I need a favour.'

The fleeting expression of delight on Scott's face was not lost on her.

'You know those photos you were showing us? The ones of you in America?'

Scott nodded.

'I don't suppose – well, could I have one?'

Scott's face flushed. 'You want a picture of me?' he asked eagerly.

'Well actually it's for . . .' she began. She couldn't drop Tansy in it; she guessed how much this meant to her. '. . . a keepsake.' She sighed feebly.

'Sure,' he enthused. 'I'll pick one out and bring it tomorrow.'

'But I wanted to choose . . .' Jade began.

She was getting into even deeper water, but she had no choice. A close-up of Scott would be of no use whatever to Tansy.

'I could come round with them after school,' Scott suggested with a grin. 'I could nip home, grab them and be at yours by half-past four.'

'No, I . . .' Jade began, and then paused. She'd be in

Allegra's good books, Tansy would be sorted and then maybe, just maybe, everyone would let her get on with her own life.

'OK,' she said. 'But I've got loads of work to do.'

'Me too,' said Scott cheerfully. 'We'll do it together.'

That, thought Jade, is what I was afraid you were going to say.

8.40 a.m

Brownie points

'I saw you talking to Scott,' Allegra babbled. 'So, go on. What did he say?'

'He's coming over to our place after school,' Jade said. 'Satisfied?'

'Oh yes,' breathed Allegra. 'Very.'

8.45 a.m.

Scheming

'Did Kyle call you? What did he want?' Holly panted, catching up with Tansy by the corner of the Sports Hall. 'What was so important he couldn't tell me? Did he ask you out? Well, go on, tell me.'

'If you stop ranting for half a second, I will,' replied Tansy with a grin. 'He's coming over to my place tonight.'

'He's what? You can't do that! What about Andy?'

'What about him?' shrugged Tansy. 'It's hardly going to

affect his life, is it?' She grinned at Holly. 'Especially since Kyle's bringing his mum with him,' she said, laughing.

'His mum?'

'Oh, Holly, stop repeating everything I say,' giggled Tansy. 'Kyle's mum is a gardener, right? Apparently, she's got herself into some sort of mess with work and can't cope, and Kyle phoned to ask whether my mum would help her out.'

'So why couldn't his mum phone herself?' Holly asked, eyeing Tansy suspiciously.

'Because of the Henry issue,' Tansy explained. 'Kyle's mum was with Henry for a year, remember, before he got it together with my mother. Trudie – that's his mum – thought she'd be the last person my mum would want to see.'

'Dead right,' Holly muttered.

'Thing is, Kyle says his mother is in a right state, so he decided to phone and see if Mum could hack it.'

'And your mum said it was OK?'

Tansy chewed her lip. 'I don't know. I haven't told her.'

'Ah.'

'I couldn't risk her saying no,' admitted Tansy. 'The way I see it, Mum gets the chance to blast off about Henry to someone other than me, you get to come round and see Kyle . . .'

'Oh my God, I hadn't thought of that!'

'I gathered,' said Tansy, sighing. 'And I get the air time to find out about . . .' She paused.

'About what?' demanded Holly.

'There's the bell for registration,' gabbled Tansy. 'I'll tell you later.'

8.55 a.m.
Photo phobia

'You're a star!' Tansy gave Jade a hug. 'So can I come and collect it tonight? I might need to escape from home.'

'Tansy, you owe me one, right?'

'Sure.'

'And if anyone's going to need an escape route from home, it's me. I'll bring them over about five-thirty, OK?'

8.58 a.m.
Little white lies

'Mum says can you call round this afternoon and collect your jacket?' Andy muttered to Tansy in registration. 'And you didn't take her anorak back.'

'Sorry,' Tansy said. 'I forgot.' Probably because, she thought, I stuffed it in the back of my locker so that no one would think it was anything to do with me. 'I'll take it after school,' she told him. 'Sorry about last night – Mum wasn't feeling well.'

'Is she better? Could I come tonight?'

'No,' Tansy replied hastily. 'She's still poorly. Sorry.'

10.00 a.m.

'Your science homework, if you please, Holly Vine.' Mr Grubb held her gaze at the start of the biology lesson.

Holly pulled a Rexel folder from her school bag and thrust it at him. 'It's not very good,' she began.

'No need to state the obvious, Holly,' returned Mr Grubb. 'At least it's here, which is a start.'

11.00 a.m.

'Will you come round and do my hair tonight?' Cleo asked Holly at the end of English. 'I've bought this amazing stuff – metallic copper highlights.'

Good grief, thought Holly.

'So will you?'

'Not tonight,' replied Holly. 'Tomorrow, OK?'

'OK, but we've got to do it then,' Cleo insisted. 'I've only got a week.'

'A week for what?' asked Holly.

'To change my entire image, silly,' Cleo persisted. 'Mum's found out that the TV people want an ordinary-looking, really last-year-type teenager.'

'Well, that's what you are,' Holly remarked. 'That is, I didn't mean . . .'

'Precisely,' interrupted Cleo. 'So if I become totally over-the-top trendy, I'll look dead classy and they won't choose me. Sorted!'

'Cleo,' remarked Holly. 'You're mad.'

11.05 a.m.

Oh sugar, thought Tansy. I've just thought – Holly's coming over to see Kyle, and Jade's coming over with the photo, and if Holly sees the photo, she'll ask questions, probably in a loud voice and probably in front of Mum. And no way must Mum find out. Not yet.

'Hey, Jade! Over here!'

11.10 a.m.

'I won't say a word, I promise,' Jade assured Tansy for the third time. 'But if it does turn out to be your dad, you'll tell your mum then, won't you?'

Tansy sighed. 'I don't dare think that far ahead,' she admitted. 'I mean, even if this guy's got a scar . . .'

'Your dad had a scar?'

Tansy nodded. 'On his forehead,' she said. 'But I guess loads of men get scars, what with playing rugby and things like that.'

'Yes, but a guy with a scar and the right name . . .'

'His name!' Tansy gasped. 'I don't know his name.'

'Your father's?' Jade asked incredulously.

'No, stupid. It's Pongo. That's what Mum calls him, anyway. I mean, the guy in the photo!' She banged the palm of her hand against her forehead. 'How could I be so dumb?'

'You mean, you never asked Scott?' Jade began.

'I was so stunned when I saw the photo, it never

crossed my mind,' Tansy admitted.

'Well, *ask* him,' Jade said, laughing.

'Oh sure. What do you expect me to say? "That guy who took you to the match might be my dad and by the way, what's his name?" I can't.'

'I can, though,' Jade said decisively.

'Don't tell him about . . .'

'I'm not stupid,' declared Jade. 'Trust me.'

1.10 p.m.
Detective work

'So tell me more about America,' Jade said, fixing an enthusiastic expression on her face and opening a packet of Wotsits with her teeth. 'Did you meet loads of Trig's friends and family?'

Scott nodded. 'They had a huge house-party for Christmas,' he said, biting into a cheese roll. 'I missed you, though. It didn't seem right being so far away.'

'Mmm,' Jade mumbled. 'Still, you couldn't have seen American football in Dunchester, could you? This uncle who took you, what . . .'

'A real bigmouth,' Scott replied, raising his eyebrows. 'Kept talking down to me like I was some nine-year-old kid who didn't have a clue about anything American.'

Bad start, thought Jade.

'Guess I shouldn't knock it, though,' Scott conceded, blowing crumbs from his upper lip. 'He had this private box at the stadium with his name in gold letters on the door . . .'

Jackpot! thought Jade. 'So what's his name?' She found herself holding her breath.

Scott grinned. 'You are not going to believe this,' he said. 'Patrick Onslow Goodlove. What a mouthful.'

Patrick, thought Jade. Poor Tansy – all that hoping for nothing.

'He's coming over this week, having dinner with my folks. Mum's in a right state because . . .'

Jade didn't bother listening. There was no point.

1.55 p.m.
Close encounters

'What are you doing here, Jade?' Miss Partridge asked as the registration bell rang. 'Surely you should be over in the science lab this period?'

'I was looking for Brooke Sylvester, Miss.' Jade sighed, salivating at the thought of the Mars bar she would buy once Brooke had repaid her.

'You and me both, dear,' retorted Miss Partridge. 'And when she does show up . . .'

'You mean, she's off school?' Jade asked, sugar deprivation looming large on the horizon.

'Brooke is usually off everything, sadly,' Miss Partridge said with a sigh, eyeing Jade closely. 'I didn't know you were a friend of hers.' She eyed Jade as if she had just announced that Jack the Ripper was her best buddy.

'I'm not really,' Jade admitted. 'It's just I lent her some money yesterday . . .'

'Yesterday?' repeated Miss Partridge, sniffing and hitching her skirt round her ample hips. 'Brooke wasn't at school yesterday. And she's not here today.'

Ah, thought Jade. 'No, well – it was after school,' she explained. 'Brooke bumped into me . . .'

'So she was out and about, then? Not so ill that she had to be confined to bed?'

Careful, Jade thought, wincing at Miss Partridge's sarcasm. Don't drop her in it.

'She'd had an awful nosebleed,' she gabbled. 'I guess that's why she's off today. She looked dead pale and washed out.'

Miss Partridge held Jade's gaze for what seemed like an eternity. 'Well,' she said, sighing. 'If she should happen to bump into you again, you might like to tell her that I need a sick note from home. Or else.'

Terrific, thought Jade as she headed down the corridor to the science lab. Now I need to find Brooke and warn her. Is there anyone on this entire planet who can sort their own lives out?

3.00 p.m.
The Cedars. On the telephone

'Is that Turner, Son and Milligan?' Holly's mother gripped the handset and surveyed a broken fingernail. 'I'm enquiring about The Laurels, Weston Way.'

She paused while the girl at the other end shuffled a few papers. 'Yes, I know it's been sold,' she went on. 'I just wondered whether you could tell me how much it fetched? What do you mean, you're not allowed? I'm a town councillor.'

She knew it would work. It always did. But as the girl whispered a figure down the phone, she felt her knees buckle.

'Sorry,' she squeaked. 'Can you repeat that? I don't think I heard correctly.' She gulped. 'No, no – there's nothing else you can help me with. Yet.'

She replaced the handset and hugged herself. 'Rupert, my darling,' she murmured to her absent husband, 'we are sitting on a little gold mine.'

3.35 p.m.
Exhibit Number One . . .

Tansy glanced over her shoulder, opened her locker and pulled out Andy's mum's jacket.

'What is *that*?' Holly appeared from the girls' toilets, looking puzzled.

'Shut it,' Tansy warned her. 'Andy's baby brother

threw up all over my coat yesterday, his mum insisted on lending me this and I forgot to take it back.'

'I don't wonder,' Holly said, laughing. 'Now I know why you looked so cold yesterday – hypothermia was a small price to pay!' She shrugged her arms into her own jacket. 'Do you want to walk home?' she queried. 'Or are you waiting for loverboy?'

'He's got orchestra practice,' Tansy told her, glaring at the hideous jacket. 'This is ever so crumpled – do you think she'll notice?'

'Like, yes.' Holly nodded. 'Give it here.' She grabbed it, turned it inside out and shook it vigorously.

'Careful!' Tansy urged. 'Now look . . .'

The contents of an inside pocket fell to the floor.

'Cute key-ring,' said Holly, stooping to pick it up. 'Look, it's got the twins' picture. Here, stuff it back in the pocket. Tansy?'

Tansy was staring at a piece of paper that had fallen out with the key-ring. Her eye were widening by the second.

'What is it?' Holly peered over her shoulder. '*Darling,*' she read out loud. '*Here's a little memento of our beautiful babies. Can't wait to see you.*'

'Sssh!' hissed Tansy. 'Keep your voice down!'

'*Wish things were different. Your Val.*'

Holly stared at Tansy. Tansy stared back at Holly.

'It's probably for Andy's dad,' said Holly softly.

'Sure.' Tansy nodded.

'Not,' they both said at once.

3.50 p.m.

'So she knows,' murmured Tansy.

'Knows what?' asked Holly.

'Who the babies' dad is,' replied Tansy.

'Well, she would, wouldn't she?' exclaimed Holly. 'It does take two – oh gosh, sorry, Tansy. I keep forgetting you're in the same boat.'

'No, I'm not,' retorted Tansy defensively. 'At least my mum came clean in the end and told me about Pongo. They might grow up never knowing . . .'

She faltered. 'Do you think I should tell Andy's mum I found the key-ring?'

'No!' screeched Holly. 'It's her mess – let her sort it.'

'Trouble is,' said Tansy, sighing. 'Parents rarely do.'

4.00 p.m.
Relief and realisation

'Oh thank goodness!' Andy's mum opened the door and snatched her jacket from Tansy's outstretched hand. 'Funny how you miss your favourite jacket, isn't it?'

Hysterical, thought Tansy, especially when it wouldn't look out of place in a museum.

'You didn't – well, you didn't leave anything in the pockets, did you?' Andy's mum mumbled, her fingers groping anxiously around the jacket.

'No,' Tansy said, as Holly's elbow dug into her back. 'I didn't touch the pockets.'

'Great,' smiled Andy's mum. 'Here – I'll fetch your jacket; I expect you two want to be on your way, then. See you soon!' And with that the front door shut.

'Guilty.' Tansy sighed. 'Definitely guilty.'

4.30 p.m.
Sorted

'Now, this is what you've got to do,' Allegra began, puckering her lips in the mirror and layering on the lip gloss. 'When Scott arrives . . .'

'Hang on,' interrupted Jade. 'I call the shots this time, OK, Legs? Scott comes, he gives me homework stuff, then I say I've got to go out and you carry on from there, get it?'

Allegra stared at her. 'You're going out?' she gasped. 'Leaving him high and dry?'

'Uh-huh.' Jade nodded.

'Oh goody,' said Allegra.

4.55 p.m.
Getting into deep water

'P' for Patrick, thought Jade. 'ON' from Onslow, 'GO,' the first two letters of 'Goodlove' . . .

'This is the best one of me,' Scott said, edging close to Jade and resting his hand on her knee.

Jade shuffled further along the sofa and rifled through the pile of pictures. 'I love this one,' she said, grabbing one of the shots of Scott and Trig's uncle.

'That one? I'm not even looking at the camera.'

'No, but you can look sort of dreamy and . . .' The moment she had said the words, she wanted to kick herself for being so stupid.

'I'd look even dreamier,' Scott said leaning towards her, his lips dangerously close to her neck, 'if you and I could just . . .'

'Jade, darling, would you and Scott like some tea?' For once in her life, Jade could have hugged her aunt for bursting unannounced into the room. 'Flapjack? Or chocolate chip muffins?'

Jade couldn't help smiling. Her aunt always produced food when boys came to the house; she clearly thought it was a deterrent to any kind of passionate advance.

'Lovely, thanks!' Jade smiled. 'Then I've got to go out.'

'Out?' her aunt demanded, her bonhomie fading rapidly. 'You're not going anywhere, young lady. You've got homework to do.'

'We're doing it together, remember,' Scott added. 'If that's OK, Mrs Webb,' he added, giving her one of his most charming smiles.

'Excellent!' she said. 'I'll get the tea.'

'Thanks a million!' Jade turned on Scott the second her aunt had disappeared. 'Now what's Tansy going to . . .' She paused.

'Tansy?' demanded Scott. 'What's Tansy got to do with anything?'

She grabbed the photograph and stared at it. Jade eyed him closely, chewing her lip. 'Can you keep a secret?' she asked.

5.00 p.m.
3 Plough Cottages, Cattle Hill

'Mum, you are not going to slob around like that all evening, are you?' Tansy asked in alarm, as her mother came down stairs wearing tracksuit bottoms and an ancient Homer Simpson T-shirt.

'Why not?' returned her mother. 'It's not like I'm going anywhere.'

'But what if someone calls round?' demanded Tansy.

'Tansy, the only people who ever call round in the evenings are your mates,' her mother reasoned. 'And if they don't like the sight of me in my joggers, they know what they can do.'

'Suit yourself,' said Tansy with a sigh.

5.05 p.m.
Even deeper water

'So you didn't really want a picture of me?' snapped Scott. 'You just wanted to get it for Tansy, right?' His face was scarlet and his jaw was working as if he was chewing a toffee.

'Of course I wanted a photo, silly,' Jade heard herself

say. 'This one's my favourite.' She picked up one of the close-up shots of Scott and slipped it into her open school bag. 'Tansy knew I wanted a picture – that's what gave her the idea of asking me to get one for her as well.'

What else could I say? she told the nagging voice of guilt in her head. *I don't have any choice.*

'So why couldn't she ask me herself?' Scott demanded, helping himself to another chocolate muffin.

Jade sighed. 'Oh, come on. Would you blab to all your mates about something that important and risk looking an idiot if it didn't work out?'

'I guess not,' Scott said, and nodded. 'But gee – I could be the cause of Tansy finding her father! Isn't that something else?'

Why, thought Jade, *does he keep talking like someone out of a badly-written soap?*

'So, you see,' she gabbled, 'I have to go over to Tansy's with this photo.'

'Can't you give it to her tomorrow?' Scott asked. 'She hasn't ever seen the guy; waiting one more day isn't going to matter.'

'I promised,' Jade explained. 'I'm really sorry.'

'Sorry enough to let me come with you?' Scott asked, holding her gaze.

No way, thought Jade. *Allegra would kill me.*

'Tansy would kill me,' Jade said hastily. 'You know what she's like.'

'I won't say anything,' he promised. 'Besides, you need me.'

'Why?'

'Well it's obvious isn't it? I *told* you, Patrick – I mean, Pongo – is coming over this week for some conference or other.'

Jade stared at him. 'Pongo? In the UK? This week?'

Scott grinned. 'Uh-huh. Now do I get to come with you? Because there's more . . .'

'Jade! Homework! Now!' Her aunt's voice echoed from the kitchen.

'And besides, without me, your aunt won't let you go anywhere,' Scott concluded triumphantly.

5.15 p.m.

Scott-ish diplomacy in Jade's kitchen

'It's all my fault, Mrs Webb,' Scott murmured. 'Jade and I are working on this project for IT, and I left my disk at home, so we need to go to my place to finish it off.'

'Well, be quick about it,' retorted Jade's aunt, chopping carrots with increased vigour. 'And wrap up well – it's bitter out there. And Jade, I want you back for supper, seven o'clock sharp.'

'Thanks,' whispered Jade to Scott. 'I owe you one.'

Why the hell, she asked herself a millisecond later, did I say that?

5.17 p.m.

Jade's front door. Caught in the act

'Where are you going?' Allegra crashed down the stairs as Jade and Scott were putting on their jackets.

'My place,' replied Scott. 'Got stuff to do, haven't we, Jade?'

'Mmm,' Jade muttered, slipping the photo of Scott and Trig's uncle into her inside pocket and opening the front door.

'I'm going to kill you,' Allegra hissed in her ear. 'Slowly and very painfully.'

'I'll explain later,' Jade muttered back. 'It's not what you think.'

'It had better not be,' retorted Allegra.

5.20 p.m.

Dream houses

'That one would be perfect,' muttered Angela, grabbing a yellow highlighter pen and circling a picture in the *Evening Telegraph*. 'Or that – not that one, though – oh, this is rather lovely . . .'

'Mum,' queried Holly, pouring lemonade into a glass. 'What are you doing?'

'House-hunting, dear.' She thrust the paper under Holly's nose. 'What do you think of that one?' she said.

'Mum,' Holly said with a sigh. 'It's lovely, but there's one problem. It costs £300,000.'

'I know,' said Holly's mum, grinning, 'but since The Laurels has just sold for £425,000 . . .'

'Four hundred and twenty-five thousand?' gasped Holly. 'That's a fortune.'

'I know.' Her mother grinned again. 'Of course, our house isn't quite as big, and we sold off that bit of garden, and it needs painting but it's on the better side of the road and . . .'

'You mean, we might be able to have that much money?' Holly was incredulous.

'Not quite that much, but if Dad agrees to sell . . .'

'Which he won't,' said Holly, with a sigh.

'Holly, I guarantee you,' her mother beamed, 'that by the end of this week, he'll be hammering in the For Sale board with his own hands.'

'What do you know that I don't?' Holly asked.

'Numerous things, dear.' Her mother grinned. 'It's one of the few privileges of growing old. Your phone's ringing.'

Holly punched the answer button.

'Kyle's here!' Tansy hissed down the phone to Holly as the headlights of a car shone into the sitting room. 'Get round here quickly.'

'And who was that?' Holly's mother enquired suspiciously.

'Just a mate,' Holly muttered.

Five minutes later . . .

'And just where do you think you're going, young lady?'

Mrs Vine ran down the stairs as Holly was putting on her new suede boots.

'Tansy's – she's got a crisis.'

'Well, she'll just have to sort it out on her own,' her mother retorted. 'You're not going anywhere dressed like that.'

'What's wrong with it?'

'Holly, it's the middle of January. Bare midriffs are for summer.'

'So I'll change,' said Holly.

'Don't bother, because you're not going anywhere,' her mother interjected. 'You are going to do your homework.'

'I'll do it later,' objected Holly.

'*Now,*' replied her mother. 'You spend far too much time finding excuses not to study.'

'But Mum, Tansy . . .'

'When it's done, I'll think about letting you pop round for a bit,' her mother conceded, as if she were conferring a special honour on her daughter.

'That'll be too late,' Holly gasped.

'It's going to be a short-lived crisis then, is it?' remarked her mother. 'Upstairs. Work. Now.'

5.27 p.m.
Tansy's house

'Get that, Tansy!' yelled her mother as the doorbell rang. 'I'm trying a new recipe.'

That's all I need, thought Tansy, dropping the handset on to the sideboard. The old ones are bad enough. She opened the front door.

'Hi, Tansy!' Kyle, a Dunchester College scarf wrapped round his neck, was standing on the doorstep stamping his feet in the cold, and tossing car keys from one hand to the other. 'Good to see you – this is my mum.'

He gestured to the tall, raven-haired woman standing beside him, wrapped in a vast purple, fur-trimmed cape and wearing the sort of black knee-length boots that Tansy would have killed for.

'I'm Trudie Woodward,' the woman smiled. 'It's so good of your mother to agree to see me. I thought she'd probably go ballistic at the thought.'

She might well have done, thought Tansy, had I told her. 'Of course not,' she gulped. 'Come in.'

Kyle's mother swept into the hallway and shrugged her cape from her shoulders.

'Mum!' Tansy called, and then winced as her mum appeared from the kitchen, wearing an apron with the words 'Kiss the Cook' emblazoned across the front.

She took a deep breath. 'Mum, this is Kyle – you remember him – from the wedding?'

Tansy's mum stood rooted to the spot, her mouth dropping open and a blob of tomato sauce on the end of her chin.

'And this,' Tansy went on hastily, 'is his mum, Trudie.'

Mrs Woodward stretched out a hand. 'Lovely to meet you, Clarity,' she enthused. 'Sorry we're a bit late, only Kyle's got his driving test next week and insisted on taking the wheel and honestly, by the time we'd gone round the roundabout four times . . .'

'You're – Kyle – his mum – the one . . .?' Tansy's mum wiped her hands on her apron.

'I can't tell you how much I appreciate your agreeing to see me,' Mrs Woodward cut in, much to Tansy's relief. Her mother tended to go monosyllabic in a crisis. 'To be honest, you are my last hope – no, I didn't mean it like that – but when you said I could come over I was so thrilled.'

'I never said . . .' she began, realisation dawning in her eyes. 'Tansy, did you . . .?'

'Oh no!' Mrs Woodward gasped, wheeling round to face Kyle. 'Are you telling me that you organised this without having the courtesy to talk to Clarity? How dare you . . .'

'No, honestly,' Tansy broke in. 'Don't blame him – it was me. Kyle asked if Mum would mind, I said no and pretended to check with her.'

For a moment no one spoke. They were all staring at Tansy.

'OK, so don't look at me like that!' she burst out. 'We're all agreed Henry was a total rat, yes?'

'Tansy, language,' her mother said with a gasp.

'She has a point, though,' interjected Kyle's mum. 'Pretty apt word, I'd say.'

'And,' Tansy gabbled on, turning towards her guest, 'Mum's really good at gardening and stuff, and Kyle said you needed help . . .'

'Tell me about it,' Mrs Woodward said, sighing.

'And ever since Henry . . .' Tansy went on.

'Don't speak about that man!' Mrs Woodward shuddered, holding up a hand.

'Well, since him, Mum's been moping about every day, feeling miserable . . .'

'I have not!' Tansy's mother exclaimed. 'Well, not every day, anyway.'

Tansy held her breath as a glimmer of a smile touched her mother's lips.

'You'd better sit down,' Tansy's mum said to Kyle's. 'And tell me, exactly what is going on?'

5.40 p.m.

Favours

'OK, I'll go home and cover for you,' Scott told Jade as they reached the corner of Cattle Hill.

'Cover? What do you mean?'

'Get real,' he said. 'If your aunt phones to check up

on you – and if she's anything like she used to be, she will – I'll say you're on your way home or in the loo or something.'

'That's really nice of you,' Jade said.

'So now you owe me two favours, right?' said Scott with a grin.

'Right.' Jade sighed. 'I'll do your French for you, if you like.'

'That,' grinned Scott, rolling his eyes, 'wasn't quite what I had in mind.'

I guessed as much, thought Jade. Why do I get myself into these muddles?

5.45 p.m.
Hotline to Holly

'Holly, where are you? He's here,' Tansy hissed down the phone while Kyle was in the loo. 'How long does it take you to walk five hundred metres?'

'Being allowed outside the front door would be a good start,' said Holly, sighing. 'Mum's in one of her controlling moods.'

'Oh, come on,' urged Tansy. 'When did you ever let something like a parent stop you? Hang on, he's coming back. Get here – fast.'

5.50 p.m.
The great escape

'Mum, Dad's back!' Holly offered up a silent prayer and beamed at her father as he staggered through the front door, balancing a pile of ring binders and folders in his arms.

'Don't shut the door, Holly,' he panted, his breath coming in short gasps. 'There's more in the boot.'

'I'll get them, Dad,' she smiled sweetly, slipping her arms into her fleece jacket. 'You go and sit down. You know what . . .'

'. . . the doctor said,' finished her father wryly. 'None of you is likely to let me forget it. OK, thank you, dear.'

He kicked open the kitchen door with his foot as Holly shot through the front door, down the drive and out in Weston Way, totally ignoring the open car boot.

OK, she'd be for it when she got home, but that was a chance she would have to take. Right now, getting a mouthful from her mother was as nothing compared to missing the chance to turn on all her feminine charms with Kyle Woodward.

5.51 p.m.

'I've got it!' Jade exclaimed as Tansy opened the door.

'Ssh!' Tansy urged, gesturing towards the half open door to the sitting room. 'Mum and Trudie are in there . . .'

'Trudie?' Jade frowned.

'Oh, I forgot, you don't know. She's Kyle's mum.'

'Kyle? The guy that dished the dirt on Henry?'

'Yes, him – he's in the kitchen. Come on through.'

'What are they doing here?' Jade gasped, following Tansy.

'It's a long story,' gabbled Tansy. 'Look – don't say anything about the photo till Holly gets here . . .'

'Holly's coming?' Jade felt more confused by the moment.

'She knows Kyle,' Tansy whispered, pausing at the kitchen door. 'When she comes, we'll leave them together and you can show me the photo, OK?' She pushed open the kitchen door. 'Sorry, Kyle – this is Jade. One of my mates. Jade, this is Kyle.'

'Jade, hi! Good to meet you!' Kyle dropped down from the worktop on which he had been perching and towered over Jade. 'We've just opened some cola – want some?'

'Please,' she said.

'Isn't he dishy?' Tansy hissed in her left ear, gesturing towards Kyle's pert bottom, tightly-clad in black denim as he crossed to the other side of the kitchen.

'Not my type,' Jade whispered back.

'Is anyone?' Tansy retorted with a grin.

Jade swallowed hard. Maybe there was something wrong with her; maybe she was the only fifteen-year-old in the universe who was bored with boys.

'Well, I mean he's quite . . .' she began, trying to retrieve her position, but at that moment the doorbell rang.

'That'll be Holly,' Tansy remarked, winking at Jade. 'Hang on a minute.' She disappeared out of the room.

'So are you in Tansy's year?' Kyle asked, pouring cola into a glass.

'Yes,' she replied, annoyed that she couldn't think of anything more intelligent to say. Not that she needed to impress him. But still . . .

'Are you . . .?' she began.

'Hi, Kyle – remember me? So how ya doing?' Holly burst through the door, ignored Jade and beamed at Kyle. 'Is that a Dunchester College scarf? That is so cool – what are you studying?'

'Come on,' Tansy hissed in Jade's ear. 'Leave them to it. We've got more important things to talk about.'

Jade followed Tansy out of the room. 'Are Kyle and Holly – well, you know, an item?' she demanded as they clattered up the uncarpeted stairs.

Tansy shrugged. 'Not yet,' she answered, pushing open her bedroom door, 'but if Holly has anything to do with it, they soon will be. Now come on, give me the photo!'

6.00 p.m.
Confessions

'And it just got worse and worse,' Mrs Woodward was saying to Tansy's mum over their second cup of tea. 'First of all, I had to move house – I simply couldn't stay in the place that wretched man had been. Don't you feel like that?' She glanced round the cluttered sitting room.

'I can't afford to move,' Tansy's mother admitted. 'Besides, Henry never lived here. He was about to move in when . . .' She faltered. Thinking about it was bad enough; putting it into words made her feel such a naïve fool. 'So what happened next?' she coaxed, keen to hear whether Kyle's mum had been duped as badly.

Trudie took a deep breath. 'I thought coming here would be a fresh start, and I took on all this new work to try to recoup some of the money Henry had conned out of me,' she began. 'But then . . .' She faltered, close to tears.

'I've really messed up,' Mrs Woodward finished. 'I've got two big contracts – both due to be completed by the end of March and there's no way on earth I can do it. Unless . . .' She chewed her lip and looked at Tansy's mother. 'What do you know about roof gardens?' she asked.

6.02 p.m.

'Rupert, what do you think the Laurels fetched?' Holly's mother began as her husband sank into the nearest chair to catch his breath.

Her husband shrugged. 'Two hundred and twenty-five thousand – quarter of a million, at a push,' he suggested.

'No dear, £425,000,' said his wife, smiling.

'What? Oh, come on, dear, you've obviously got it wrong.'

'I have not,' Mrs Vine declared. 'And do you know what? The agents think we could get at least £395,000 for this place even with the . . .'

'Angela, how many times do I have to tell you?' her husband cut in. 'This place was built by my grandfather and I promised my father that I'd look after The Cedars, keep it in the family, bequeath it to the next generation . . .'

'Darling, I hardly think Holly will want . . .'

'Not Holly,' Mr Vine corrected her. 'But Richard or Tom might like it.'

'I think,' his wife, sighing, 'they'd prefer a hole in the head. And besides, it's costing a bomb heating all those empty rooms now the boys have gone.'

'Angela, for the last time . . .'

'OK, OK, if you say so.'

'I do,' he asserted. 'Where's Holly gone? She's got the rest of my stuff.'

6.05 p.m.

In Tansy's bedroom

'Do you think it's him?'

Jade could hear the anxiety in Tansy's voice as she shoved the two photographs under her nose.

'See – this one was taken before I was born and this is him now.' Jade looked from one picture to the other.

'That mark there,' Tansy babbled on, pointing to the new photo. 'That could be a scar.'

As she passed the photo to Jade, it slipped from her hands and fell on to the floor.

'Hey, wait,' she cried, stooping down to pick it up. 'There's something written on the back.' She scanned Scott's scrawl and her face fell. 'It's not him.' She shoved the photo into Jade's hands. 'Look.'

'*Patrick and me at the football game*,' Jade read.

'Patrick.' Tansy sighed, swallowing hard.

'Yes, but Patrick is Pongo, I'm sure of it!' Jade cut in, unable to contain herself any longer. 'Scott told me that he's called Patrick Onslow Goodlove III.'

'So?'

Jade grinned at Tansy. 'You don't get it, do you?' she urged. '"P" for Patrick, add "ON" from Onslow and . . .'

'"GO" from Goodlove and you've got Pongo!' Tansy's voice cracked with emotion. 'Jade, you're brilliant. Could it be? Do you really think it could be?' A tear trickled down her cheek. 'Sorry,' she said, turning away and rubbing her cheek with the back of her hand.

'It's OK,' Jade assured her, giving her a hug. 'I reckon you're allowed to cry when you've just discovered a dad.' She paused and gave Tansy a hug. 'And any day now you might actually get to meet him.'

6.10 p.m.
Job opportunities

'Me? Work with you?' Tansy's mum stared at Kyle's mother in disbelief.

'I guess it was dumb idea,' Mrs Woodward said, sighing and getting to her feet. 'I suppose seeing me would keep reminding you of Henry and besides, you probably like being on your own, doing your own thing . . .'

'I've had enough of going it alone to last me a lifetime,' Tansy's mum confessed. 'When do we start?'

6.15 p.m.

'What are you on about?' Tansy gasped. 'Pongo coming to England? How do you know?'

'Scott said that . . .'

'Scott said . . .? You told Scott about me and Pongo?' Tansy exploded. 'Jade, how could you? You promised.'

Jade swallowed. 'Tansy, I'm sorry, I had no choice . . .'

'Oh, sure you had a choice!' Tansy stormed, a sob catching in her throat. 'How could you be so . . .?'

'Just a minute,' Jade retorted, raising her voice. 'Who

was it who worked out that this Patrick guy and Pongo are one and the same? Who walked round here in the freezing cold to give you the wretched photograph when I could have made you wait till tomorrow? Who is about to tell you . . .?' She stopped as Tansy burst into tears.

'I know, I know, I'm sorry,' Tansy said, weeping. 'I just feel all muddled and confused and chewed-up inside. Like, I always dreamed that I'd find him, but now that I actually might – well, I don't know what to do.'

'Listen,' Jade said, putting an arm round her shoulder. 'It just slipped out with Scott – but then he said that Pongo's coming to a conference. Do you want me to find out the details or not?'

Tansy nodded. 'Could you? I don't know why, but I feel I just can't put all this into words right now.'

'I'll talk to him tomorrow, OK? Now can we go downstairs?'

'Why?'

'No reason.'

6.22 p.m.

'Holly dear, your mother's on the phone,' Tansy's mum called, following Jade and Tansy into the kitchen and grabbing a bottle of white wine from the fridge. 'She doesn't sound terribly happy.'

'Ah,' said Holly. 'Tell her I've just left, will you? Please?'

Tansy's mother eyed her closely. 'If I wasn't in such a

good mood, I'd have to come clean with your mum,' she teased. 'OK, leave it to me – but run, OK?'

Tansy stared at her mother. Not only was she colluding with Holly, but she was smiling from ear to ear.

Holly turned to Jade. 'We've sorted your party probs, Kyle and me,' she said. 'He'll fill you in.'

'What do you mean?'

Holly ignored her and turned to Kyle. 'See you Saturday, then,' she murmured seductively. 'Can't wait.'

6.22 p.m.

'What's with all this stuff about seeing Holly on Saturday?' Tansy demanded of Kyle. 'It's Jade's party that day.'

'I know.' Kyle nodded. 'Holly told me. And she said you're wanting a disco, right?'

Jade shrugged. 'I don't actually want a party,' she began. 'I'm not really a party-type person.'

'Oh,' Kyle said with a frown. 'So you don't want me?'

'Want you?' Jade croaked.

'I do this mobile disco thing with my mate, Angus,' he began. 'Kick Ass, it's called. Holly said you'd been desperate to find someone and I said we could do it really cheaply at your house. But I guess if you're not up for it . . .'

'I am,' Jade burst out. If I tried really hard, I could fancy him. I'm sure I could. I am, really. A disco is just what I wanted. How much does it cost?'

6.35 p.m.

Not that he's dishy or anything

There is, thought Jade, fingering the piece of paper with Kyle's phone number on it as she walked home from Tansy's, just the small point of persuading her aunt. But then again, if Allegra's so keen to have Scott, she can do the persuading. She's better at it than me. Of course I'll have to get something new to wear. Black satin trousers, maybe, and one of those glitzy tops that clings in all the right places.

'Shut it, will you?'

Jade's musings were interrupted by a frantic shout from the other side of the road. If it had not been for the glare of a street lamp, she might not have recognised the girl huddling in the bus shelter.

'Hey, Brooke!' she called.

She was with three other girls, and Jade was pretty sure that at least one of them had been in the group that had been bullying her the day before.

'Brooke! Over here!'

'So just shut up and leave me alone!' she heard Brooke yell at the girls.

The tall one made a rude gesture and stuck out her tongue. 'Bog off!' She sneered, as Brooke broke into a run and crossed over the road. 'And don't forget what I said, wimp!'

'Are you OK?' Jade asked as Brooke fell into step beside her. 'You shouldn't go near those girls if that's the way they treat you.'

Brooke shrugged. 'They kind of hang about, waiting for me,' she admitted. 'Every day.' She looked at Jade with huge grey eyes. 'It's horrible.'

'Have you told someone?' Jade asked her. 'What about your parents?'

Brooke quickened her pace. 'What about them?' she retorted. 'I sort myself out.'

Jade's heart went out to her. Suddenly she didn't look fourteen; more like a very scared eleven.

'Look,' Jade suggested, 'why don't you tell Miss Partridge? She was asking me about you only today – she said you'd been off school and . . .'

'What did you say?' Brooke snapped back.

'Don't worry,' Jade reassured her. 'I said you'd had a really bad nosebleed and looked dreadful.'

Brooke eyed her cautiously. 'You covered for me? Thanks!' She sounded genuinely surprised.

'You'll have to show up tomorrow, though,' Jade went on. 'She's on the warpath.'

'So what's new?' muttered Brooke. 'She hates me.'

'Don't be daft,' Jade laughed. 'She's a softie. She might sound fierce, but she's always fair.'

'And what would you know about it?' Brooke demanded. 'Straight As for everything, never put a foot wrong . . .'

'I ran away once,' Jade said, 'and Birdie was really cool.'

'You did?' Brooke looked impressed. 'Why? When?'

Jade wished she hadn't said anything. She was doing her best to forget the past and move on. 'Oh, it was after my parents died . . . anyway, tell her about the girls, right?' she urged, slowing down as she neared her house.

'She can't do anything about them,' Brooke told her. 'They don't go to West Green – they're none of her business.' She shivered and pulled her flimsy denim jacket more tightly round her body. 'Anyway, I'm OK. Hey, is this where you live?' She gestured to number fifty-three.

Jade nodded. 'What about you?'

'Frimley Rise,' she said, gesturing over the rooftops of the houses to the estate behind. 'Only till . . .' She stopped.

'Till what?'

'What's with all the questions?' Brooke snapped. 'What is it to you?'

'Nothing.' Jade sighed. 'Oh, and can I have my five pounds, please? I don't get my allowance till next week.'

'Oh get you,' retorted Brooke. '*I don't get my allowance till next week*. Like, I should be so lucky.' She sniffed and dropped her eyes. 'I haven't got your money,' she said. 'My mum wouldn't give it me – when I asked she just lost it with me and . . .'

'Oh, Brooke, look, I'm sorry, forget it,' Jade gabbled. 'It's OK, really.'

'Are you sure?' Brooke looked anxious. 'I mean, I'll ask again in a couple of days.'

'No,' said Jade firmly. 'Let it go. I'll see you tomorrow, yes?'

A thought crossed her mind. 'How about I meet you at the corner and walk to school?' she offered. 'Those girls . . .'

'OK, then!' Brooke's face broke into a smile. 'That'd be cool.'

Jade waved as she slipped her key into the front door. I'm getting good at sorting people out, she thought. Now all I have to do is get Scott to cough up the information about this conference, pair him off with Allegra, get Brooke to talk to Miss Partridge and then I can concentrate on me.

Would a denim mini be better than trousers, I wonder?

6.50 pm.

'Mum?' Tansy began.

'Mmm,' her mother murmured, pulling open the fridge door.

'You know Pongo?' Tansy held her breath.

'What about him?'

'Funny name to give a kid, wasn't it?' she remarked, her heart pounding in her ears.

'It was a nickname, silly,' her mother said. 'He never used his real name.'

'Which was?' She could actually hear her heart beating in her ears.

'Look, do we have to keep bringing up the subject of your father? He's in the past. Over. Done with.'

'I just wondered, that's all,' Tansy murmured.

'He was named after his dad, he hated his dad, so he refused to use the name, OK?' Clarity sighed. 'Anyway, Pongo's a much funkier name than Patrick, isn't it?'

6.55 p.m.
In shock

It's him, Tansy repeated to herself for the tenth time. I've found my dad. No one would believe it – it's like one of those silly stories on TV where people go 'Oh puh-leese!' when something unlikely happens.

But it *has* happened, she thought. I think I'm going to cry. Or be sick. Or both.

7.05 p.m.

'So, Mum, about Jade's party,' Allegra began over supper. 'She fancies . . .'

'I've found this dead-cheap disco called Kick Ass,' Jade cut in.

'Called what?' Her aunt looked as if she was about to pass out.

'Kickers,' Jade improvised hastily. 'They come to your house and . . .'

'A disco? Here at the house?

Why, thought Jade, do adults have to repeat everything you say?

'Of course it's OK, right, Mum?' Allegra said, eyeing her cousin with unusual admiration. 'We can have the music in the conservatory and dance in the sitting room and we'll order pizzas so you don't have to do food. You won't have to worry about a thing.'

'But this disco,' her aunt murmured. 'Who are these Kick people? I don't know a thing about them.'

'They're friends of Tansy's mum,' Jade announced and was gratified to see that her punchline had actually brought a relaxed smile to her aunt's face.

7.07 p.m.

'Mum – you're singing again,' Tansy commented, as she came out of the bathroom after washing her face. 'So what's with this new job with Trudie?'

'Roof gardens,' her mother said, beaming. 'It's brilliant, you see – there are these hotels and offices that want all year round places for dinners and parties and such like, glazed over in the winter, open air in summer, and I've been thinking that if we planted some . . .'

'OK, OK.' Tansy laughed. 'I don't need the details. I'm just pleased to have my old Mum back.'

'You know, I even feel in the mood for cooking something really exotic,' her mum said, beaming. 'I think I'll make us my seaweed risotto for supper.'

'There is,' replied Tansy, 'a downside to everything.'

10.30 p.m.
Trying it on again

'You'll have to do something about it, Angela,' Mr Vine said, climbing into bed.

'About what, dear?

'The Laurels. It's no place for a garden centre – all those people driving up at the weekends, blocking the road – I can't think how they got planning permission . . .'

'Darling, don't distress yourself,' his wife urged him, patting his arm. 'It's not a flower nursery. It's a kids' nursery. You know, babies and stuff.'

'Babies? Yelling kids? In Weston Way?' He stared at her, open-mouthed. 'We can't allow that – it'll lower the tone – and besides, the noise and . . .'

'It's a much needed facility,' his wife replied. 'So many single mums and working parents . . .'

'Yes, but . . .'

'Not in your back yard, is that it?' She sighed. 'Well, my darling love, there is one thing I could do to help you.'

'What's that? One of your protest marches? Letter to the *Telegraph*?'

'No, my angel,' his wife said with a smile, snuggling down under the duvet. 'Start house hunting.'

Her husband snorted and said nothing. But nothing, Mrs Vine thought to herself, was a step in the right direction.

WEDNESDAY

4.00 a.m.

3 Plough Cottages, Cattle Hill. Dream on

'Tansy! Darling – I've been searching for you all my life,' Pongo cried.

'Me too,' Tansy shouted running into his arms.

Pongo turned into a pile of pink laundry and Tansy woke up.

5.00 a.m.

Tossing and turning

Don't think about him, Tansy told herself, thumping her pillow. Just go back to sleep.

5.30 a.m.

Creative visualisation

What if she did meet him? What would she say?

'Hi, I'm your daughter – the one you never bothered about . . .'

'Hi, I'm Tansy and I know you must regret not ever coming to see me so I've come to you and . . .'

She sighed and rolled over on to her stomach. Chances are the conference would be somewhere like Edinburgh and she'd never get to see him, anyway.

8.00 a.m.

'And where are you dashing off to?' Allegra asked. 'You're not meeting . . .'

'Not Scott.' Jade sighed. 'Brooke Sylvester.'

'Brooke?' gasped Allegra. 'That no-hoper?'

'That is so judgemental,' snapped Jade. 'You don't even know the girl.'

'I know she's always on report or in detention,' sneered Allegra. 'I wouldn't have thought a goody-goody like you would go within a million miles of her.'

'Actually,' retorted Jade, 'I'm thinking of inviting her to my party. I think she's got problems.'

'Oh, and Miss Jade Good Samaritan Williams is going to sort them, right?'

'Someone has to fight her corner,' Jade declared.

Allegra shook her head. 'Get friendly with that kid, and you'll be the one who needs sorting,' she declared.

8.10 a.m.

Crawling, grovelling and generally conniving

'. . . And as a result of your deception, you are grounded for one week,' Mrs Vine shouted at Holly, dumping breakfast dishes into the dishwasher.

'That is so not fair!' Holly gasped, gulping down the dregs of her orange juice. 'It's Jade's party on Saturday.'

'You should have thought of that . . .'

'But I only went round the corner to Tansy's – you

make it sound like I skived off school or something.'

'Where you went is not the point,' her father butted in, biting into his toast and honey. 'Your mother had specifically told you that your homework took priority.'

Got it, thought Holly, as an idea shot into her mind. She summoned up every ounce of dramatic talent within her and forced a couple of tears into her eyes. She added a little gulp for extra effect and sniffed audibly.

'That's the whole point,' she said, forcing a sob into her voice. 'I went to Tansy's to get help with my science because I can't do it and . . .'

She paused, put her hands to her face, rubbed her right eye and looked pleadingly at her father. He was always a softer touch than her mum.

'Dad, I've made an awful mess of my options,' she murmured. 'And I can't cope with the work, and I knew if I got low grades I'd be letting you down, so I thought if I just dashed round to Tansy's and . . .' She was running out of breath but fortunately her father cut in.

'Hey, Hollyberry,' he began.

Good sign, thought Holly triumphantly. He only calls me Hollyberry when he's feeling paternal.

'If you've got a problem, come to Mum or me,' he went on. 'We can help.'

'Mum's useless at science,' Holly said, sniffing, 'and you . . .' This should do it. ' . . . you've been ill and I didn't want to worry you.'

'That's sweet of you, darling,' her father said, smiling. 'Isn't that sweet, Angela?'

'Unbelievably sweet,' muttered her mother, flicking the switch on the dishwasher and glancing sceptically at her daughter.

'I've been so scared of telling you,' Holly added for good measure.

'Well you must promise to come to us with your worries in future,' her father insisted. 'Promise?'

'I promise,' Holly said. 'So – er – about being grounded . . .?'

'I think,' murmured her father, 'that perhaps your mother overreacted.'

Holly didn't hang around for the explosion she just knew was about to take place.

8.15 a.m.
Shock

'Hang on,' said Brooke as she and Jade reached the corner shop. 'I want some crisps. Coming?'

While Brooke rifled through the piles of crisps and sweets on the counter, Jade picked up a copy of *Flourish!* and flicked through the pages. A miniskirt, definitely, she thought, with striped socks, or maybe legwarmers – but then again . . .

'Are you buying that or not?' The assistant glared at her over the counter. 'You kids, you're all the same, fingering the goods . . .'

'Come on!' Brooke grinned, waving a packet of

crisps in her face. 'Let's shoot!'

Jade slipped the magazine back onto the rack and followed Brooke into the street, pulling her scarf round her neck as the wind whipped round the corner.

'Crisp?' Brooke said, shoving the packet at her. 'Or chocolate?' She pulled a Flake, a Mars bar and a bag of Maltesers from her school bag.

'I've only just had breakfast.' Jade laughed. 'And hey – if you had enough cash to pay for that lot, I should have demanded my five pounds.'

'Who said,' sneered Brooke, 'that I paid for them?'

8.30 a.m.
Revelations

'If you're going to get on your high horse, you can get lost!' Brooke shouted after Jade had spent five minutes laying into her about stealing.

'But you stole them – it's just not on,' Jade insisted, slackening her pace as they reached the school gates. Maybe Allegra was right; maybe Brooke really was bad news.

'Oh, and getting beaten up is, is that it?' Brooke spat. 'Not that you'd know . . .'

'Beaten up?' Jade gasped. 'You mean, those girls . . .?'

'I'm not saying anything, OK?' Brooke retaliated. 'And if you say I did . . .'

'OK, so I won't say a word,' Jade assured her, anxious

to get the full story. 'But did they? Put you up to it, I mean?'

Brooke hesitated. 'They get me to do stuff,' she said. 'And if I don't it, they say they'll tell everyone.'

'Tell everyone what?' she asked, straining to catch her words against the background of speeding traffic.

'That my dad's in prison,' she whispered.

8.35 a.m.

Feeling needed

I knew I was right, Jade assured herself. She's not bad. She's just had a tough time of it. She needs a friend. Someone steady and solid. Someone like me. Maybe I won't be a nurse. Maybe I'll be a social worker.

Meanwhile, in the park . . .

'You know when your mum went missing?' Tansy began, kicking at some dried leaves as she and Andy crossed the park to school.

'We don't talk about that any more,' Andy retorted. 'It's in the past . . .'

'I know, it's just that . . . well, what if she hadn't come back and . . .'

'She did, and it's over!' Andy spat back. 'Now shut it, will you?'

Fine, thought Tansy. I won't tell you then.

8.42 a.m.

Guy ratings

'Did Kyle mention me after I'd gone?' Holly demanded of Tansy.

'No,' she said. 'Oh, yes actually. He said that you'd been talking about Jade's party on Saturday and she told him she didn't want a disco.'

'She what? She's got to have one. I've got it all planned,' Holly cried.

'It's OK,' grinned Tansy. 'When Jade found out Kyle was the DJ, she changed her tune so fast you wouldn't believe it.'

'Oh good - what? You don't mean - Jade doesn't fancy him, does she?'

'With Jade, you can never tell.' Tansy sighed. 'She says she doesn't like boys but . . .'

'Good,' said Holly. 'Let's hope it stays that way.'

9.00 a.m.

In registration. The hand of Fate

'Scott, listen. I need to talk to you,' Jade began, dumping her school bag on the table. 'Tansy reckons that guy in the picture is you-know-who.' She dropped her voice. 'And I wondered - when he sees your parents . . .

'He says he can't take them out,' Scott said. 'Too many work commitments or something.'

Jade's heart sank.

'My mum's dead miffed.' He grinned. 'She fancied a posh dinner at Staverton Lakes.'

Jade's mouth dropped open. Staverton Lakes was the new swish hotel and conference complex on the edge of town; Tansy could be within a couple of miles of her long-lost father.

'Are you sure?' she insisted. 'He's staying at Staverton Lakes?' She shook her head. 'Coincidences like that just don't happen,' she said, sighing.

'Coincidences,' Scott said, grinning again, 'are just miracles in which God decides to remain anonymous. I read that on a poster at Chicago airport. It's Fate – Tansy's meant to meet him.'

He punched Jade's arm. 'He's at the conference till Sunday,' he said.

'Scott, you're a star,' Jade told him.

'So do I get a snog?' he asked, sidling up to her.

'Got to go – must find Tansy,' Jade gabbled. 'Bye!'

10.15 a.m.
In geography

'Did you find out anything?' Tansy hissed urgently at Jade, while Mrs Godfrey wittered on about population growth in Northern Europe.

'Yes,' whispered Jade. She leaned across the table and whispered to Tansy.

'WHAT?' Tansy blurted out.

'Tansy Meadows,' shouted Mrs Godfrey, 'are you of the opinion that your understanding of geography is adequate to see you through GCSE with flying colours? Because I don't.'

'Sorry, Miss,' Tansy murmured dutifully.

'It's good enough to get us where we're going, though,' Jade whispered.

Meanwhile, in French . . .

'It's freezing in here,' moaned Cleo. 'My fingers are turning blue.'

'What were you saying, Cleo Greenway?' demanded Mrs Chapman.

'I said I was cold, Miss,' said Cleo.

'Well, say it in French,' retorted the teacher. 'Or keep quiet.'

11.00 a.m.

At break – stuffing her face with KitKat

'I can't believe it,' Tansy said for the third time. 'Staverton Lakes – I mean it's so close. I can . . . well, I could . . .'

'See him,' Jade finished for her. 'That is the general idea.'

Tansy's face fell. 'But there's school . . .'

'So throw a sickie,' encouraged Jade. 'I'll cover for you.'

'You,' said Tansy, 'are a star.'

11.40 a.m.
Recriminations

'Holly, this assignment was a disaster,' Mr Grubb said. 'What is wrong with you these days?'

You tell me, thought Holly. You're the one who is supposed to have all the answers.

'Don't know, Sir. Sorry, Sir.'

'Do it again, Holly – and this time use your brain.'

12 noon
At the Cedars

'Clarity, for the past month, you've had a face as long as a wet weekend,' remarked Angela Vine, opening the back door and handing Clarity a mug of coffee. Today you keep singing and talking to yourself. What's up?'

'I've got a job,' Tansy's mother beamed. 'A proper job – with Trudie.'

'And who is Trudie?'

'You remember Henry?'

'As if I could forget . . .'

'Well, Trudie's the woman he duped before moving on to me,' said Clarity. 'What happened was this . . .'

She explained the whole story to Holly's mum. 'And we are going to call ourselves True Clarity. Don't you think that's clever?'

'Mmm,' replied Mrs Vine doubtfully. 'Very original.'

12.45 p.m.
Quick thinking

'Is that Clarity? Oh, it's Paula here – Jade's aunt. Look, these friends of yours – the disco people? Are they OK?'

'Excuse me?' Tansy's mother stuck a finger in one ear and shifted her mobile into her other hand.

'Kickers,' Jade's aunt went on. 'Kyle someone or other.'

Tansy's mother's brain clicked up a gear. Tansy had muttered something about a disco party that Jade was having, and knowing how neurotic Paula Webb was, she could guess at her next question.

'Oh yes – ever such a nice boy, son of my colleague, Trudie Woodward.' She heard the sigh of relief down the phone.

'That's OK, then,' Mrs Webb replied. 'You can't be too careful these days can you?'

Meanwhile ...
At The Cedars, running up the phone bill

'Edward? It's Angela Vine here. Now look, you're on the Planning Committee, aren't you? Well, there's something I'd like you to find out for me . . .'

'Hortense? When is the next meeting of the Highways committee? Tonight? Perfect! Could you raise a question for me?'

2.05 p.m.
Waiting for biology to start

'This radiator is stone cold,' complained Holly.

'They all are.' Cleo nodded. 'I reckon we should complain.'

'That,' interjected Mr Grubb appearing behind them, 'will not be necessary. The head has called an emergency assembly. You are to be in the hall in ten minutes. Go!'

2.15 p.m.
Emergency assembly

'And so, reluctantly, I fear we are going to have to close the school and send you home until the engineers can fix the boilers.'

'YES! WOW! RESULT! NICE ONE!' The cries went up all round the hall.

'And,' continued the head, holding up a hand, 'school will remain closed tomorrow. You are all to return on Friday morning. Now, anyone who has problems with parents being at work may wait in the gym where there are some electric heaters . . .'

2.20 p.m.
Forward planning

'That's brilliant!' Cleo beamed at Holly as they trooped

downstairs. 'You can come to my place tomorrow and do my hair . . .'

'Not a clever idea,' interjected Holly. 'I thought your mum wanted you to stay just the way you are.'

'I hadn't thought of that,' gasped Cleo. 'Not to worry, I'll come to yours.'

'OK,' agreed Holly, 'Mum's out all morning doing her old people's lunches. We won't be disturbed. But there's one condition.'

'What?'

'I do your hair; you do my science, OK?'

'It won't be very good,' protested Cleo.

'It'll be better than anything I can do,' said Holly, with a sigh.

2.25 p.m.
More plans

'It's destiny, isn't it?' Tansy breathed, packing her school bag. 'I mean, when was the last time we got a day off school, just like that?'

She grabbed Jade's arm. 'Don't you see? It means I can go and find Pongo and Mum will be none the wiser. You will come with me, won't you?' she pleaded. 'I can't do it on my own.'

Tansy nodded. 'Sure, if you want me to,' she said. 'But what about Andy?'

2.28 p.m.
Alibis

'Holly!' Tansy gasped, catching up with her in the locker room. 'I need a favour. Can you pretend I'm at your house tomorrow?'

'Why?' demanded Holly.

'The thing is, I've got major plans, and I don't want Mum asking too many questions. I thought I'd pretend to be with you doing homework or something.'

'And you think your mum will swallow that one?' asked Holly.

'Sure to.' Tansy nodded.

'It must be wonderful,' remarked Holly, 'to have a gullible mother.'

2.35 p.m.

'A bunch of us are going bowling tomorrow,' Scott said casually, joining Jade and Tansy as they walked across the playground. 'Want to come?'

'I can't,' Jade replied, shaking her head. 'I'm going with Tansy to look for P . . .' She stopped, mouth half-open, and looked apologetically at Tansy.

'It's OK.' Tansy smiled. 'I wouldn't be going if it wasn't for Scott.'

'You're going to find Patrick?' Scott gasped. 'Great – I'll come with you.'

'I thought,' Jade interrupted, 'you were going bowling.'

'Not any more,' Scott said breezily. 'You need me there.'

'No, honestly . . .' Jade began.

'That's a great idea,' Tansy enthused. 'After all, Pongo knows Scott – he's far more likely to chat to me if Scott says I'm a mate. Thanks, Scott, you're a star.'

3.10 p.m.

Thanks Scott, you're a star, Jade muttered to herself, ambling along Lime Avenue towards home. I don't know why I'm bothering to go – clearly she doesn't need me now. She sighed. She'd had this vision of being the one to rush up to Pongo, grab his arm, introduce him to Tansy and watch the pair of them fall into one another's arms while telling her they would be indebted to her for life.

But it's not about me, she told herself. And besides, I will go – Scott's male and odds are, he'll mess up anyway.

'Jade! Wait!' She was jolted out of her thoughts by the sound of her name and the pounding of trainers on the pavement behind her.

'Hi!' Brooke said. 'I was looking for you at school – I've got your money.'

'You have?' Jade couldn't keep the surprise out of her voice.

'Alice gave it to me this morning,' she explained, shoving a five-pound note at Jade. 'So thanks.'

'Alice?' Jade queried.

For a long moment, Brooke said nothing. Her cheeks flushed and she chewed her lip.

'My foster mum. Any more questions?' she mumbled.

Poor girl, thought Jade. What a life. 'Actually,' she said brightly, a thought coming into her head. 'I was going to ask you if you'd like to come to my party. On Saturday.'

'Party?' Brooke repeated. 'Why would you want me at your party?'

'I'm asking loads of friends.' Jade shrugged. 'We're having a disco and food and stuff. Bring a mate or two, if you like.'

'A mate? Could I?' Brooke's eyes brightened.

'Sure,' shrugged Jade.

'Cool.' Brooke grinned. 'I think I just might do that.'

5.00 p.m.

Jade's house. Being saintly – not

'A day off?' Jade's aunt exclaimed. 'That'll give you a chance to do some serious revision.'

'I know,' Jade replied as meekly as she could. 'I'm going over to Tansy's to use her computer.'

'What's wrong with the one here?' her aunt demanded.

'Allegra will need it,' Jade answered. 'She's got so much catching up to do and it's not fair for me to hog the computer.'

'What a kind thought.'

What a bit of inspired lying, you mean, Jade thought. I'm getting rather good at improvisation.

6.30 p.m.

'Staverton Lakes Hotel and Conference Centre, Brenda speaking. How may I help you?'

Tansy gripped the handset. 'Do you have a Patrick Goodlove staying with you?' She held her breath.

'Mr Goodlove checked in an hour ago – can I put you through?'

'No, no – it's fine.' Tansy's words came out as a faint squeak. 'I'll – I wanted – I just wanted to make sure he'd arrived safely.'

7.15 p.m.
While cooking stinging-nettle soup

'Hello? Dunchester 577078 – Clarity Meadows speaking. Oh, Trudie. Hi!' She covered the mouthpiece. 'Stir the soup,' she whispered to Tansy. 'Sorry, Trudie – what? Tomorrow? Yes, sure that would be great.'

'Are we supposed to eat this?' Tansy muttered, sniffing the saucepan suspiciously.

'Be quiet,' her mother hissed. 'No, Trudie, not you – Tansy's wittering on.'

'Charming,' muttered Tansy.

'Yes, I'll pick you up at eight-thirty. Can't wait. *Ciao!*'

'What's happening tomorrow?' Tansy asked anxiously.

'My first day as half of True Clarity,' her mother said, grinning. 'I've got a really good feeling about this, Tansy.'

'Good,' replied Tansy. 'I wish I could say the same about the soup.'

8.25 p.m.
Strategic planning

'Tansy? It's Scott. Listen, about tomorrow . . .'

'Don't tell me you're not coming?'

'Of course I'm coming. Just make sure you come in school uniform . . .'

'Uniform? On a day off – get real!'

Tansy heard Scott sighing down the phone. 'Trust me, OK?' he urged. 'It could be the one way of making sure Pongo gives you a load of airtime.'

'Sure? OK, then. But I don't get it.'

'You will,' Scott promised her. 'I'll phone Jade and tell her the same thing. I feel like an MI5 spy.'

10.00 p.m.
53 Lime Avenue. Getting ready for bed

'What are you doing tomorrow?' Allegra asked Jade as they passed one another on the landing.

'Going out with Tansy and Scott.' The words were out before Jade's brain clicked in.

'Scott? You can't do that, you promised, you said . . .'

'*You* said that you wanted me to chat Scott up all week and then be horrid at the party,' Jade reminded her. 'That's what I'm doing. OK?'

Allegra eyed her closely. 'And you swear on your life you don't fancy him?' she demanded. 'Not even a bit.'

'No way,' Jade said. 'I'm doing all this for you.'

'OK,' she said. 'But just keep the chatting up low-key, right?'

THURSDAY

9.15 a.m.

On the bus to Staverton Lakes

'I feel sick,' Tansy groaned, wrapping her arms round her stomach. 'What shall I say to him?'

'How about, "Hi, I'm Tansy and I think you're my dad?"' Jade suggested.

'Oh, like that's really tactful,' Tansy spluttered, fingering the photo of Pongo that she had slipped into her jacket pocket. 'I can't afford to get it wrong. It's OK for you, you're not about to meet your long lost dad and . . . oh, my God, Jade, I'm sorry.'

Jade swallowed hard, an image of her dead father swimming in front of her eyes. 'Actually,' she said, gazing at Tansy, 'out of the two of us, I reckon you've got it easy.'

9.25 a.m.

Scott was waiting for them outside the hotel as they ran up, faces pinched from the cold wind blowing across the landscaped gardens.

'The place is heaving,' he told them, as they pushed through the revolving doors into the foyer of the hotel. Clusters of men and women with briefcases and folders were talking in animated fashion under a sparkling chandelier.

'Jade, look – over there!' Tansy pointed to a display board. '*Staverton Lakes Hotel welcomes delegates to the YummyScrum conference*,' she read.

'YummyScrum,' exclaimed Jade. 'Aren't they the people that make all those gorgeous waffles and funny-shaped doughnuts? The ones with the three aliens on the TV ad?'

'Mmm,' murmured Tansy. 'The ones my mother calls filthy junk and refuses to buy.'

'Right,' Scott hissed at them, as they reached the reception desk. 'Here goes.'

Tansy took a deep breath and prayed hard.

'Excuse me,' Scott began, in a rather more upmarket voice than his friends were used to hearing, 'but can you tell me if Mr Patrick Goodlove is available?'

The bored-looking receptionist, wearing a badge which read *'I'm Miranda – Here to Help You'* ran a scarlet-varnished finger down the register.

'He is a guest here, yes,' she said. 'Shall I call his room?'

'Yes, please,' said Scott.

They waited.

'No reply,' Miranda remarked, glancing at the clock above the desk. 'It's gone nine-thirty – I guess he's in the conference room.'

'Oh good,' Scott said. 'So where do we go?'

'You can't just go barging in,' Miranda retorted. 'It's delegates only.'

'I know that.' Scott smiled, waving his notebook in her face. 'But we're the group from West Green Academy, you know?' He pointed to the badge on Tansy's blazer and winked at her. 'We're the ones sent to do the "Youth meets Business" interviews.'

Miranda looked about as interested as if Scott was reading the weather forecast to her. 'Hackleton Suite,' she yawned. 'Take the lift to the fourth floor, turn right, through the double doors and it's the first room on the left.'

'Thank you so much,' said Scott, moving away. He grinned at Jade and Tansy, who were staring at him open-mouthed. 'So come on,' he beckoned. 'What are you waiting for?'

9.45 a.m.
Make it up as you go along

'It looks a bit complicated,' Cleo admitted, perching on the edge of the bath and scanning her eyes over the instruction leaflet in the Glint 'n' Gleam Hi-lite pack.

'It'll be fine,' Holly replied airily, taking the packet from her hands and glancing at it. 'Oh good grief!'

'What?' demanded Cleo.

'Are you sure this is quite you?' Holly ventured, pulling the plastic cap from the box.

'Yes, I'm sure,' returned Cleo, thrusting a sheet of paper under her nose. 'I found this amazing website – Makeover Sorted – where you put your face shape in and then try out hair and lips and stuff.'

Holly's eyes widened as she looked at the picture. 'It's a bit dramatic,' she murmured, eyeing the bottles of highlighter. 'Bronze Bonanza and Silver Shindig – and you want them both? Are you sure?'

'Look at me,' Cleo replied with a sigh. 'I've looked like this since I was eleven. I've always played safe and I'm sick of it. Besides, if I go really trendy, I won't have to make a fool of myself on TV – and my mother will learn that she can't always have her own way.'

'OK, it's your call,' shrugged Holly. 'Let's get highlighting.'

10.00 a.m.
First sightings

'That's him, over there!' Scott whispered to Tansy as a tall man in a purple shirt and grey suit mounted the podium.

Tansy couldn't speak. She couldn't think straight. This really was it.

'Excuse me.' A plump woman wearing a lurid pink badge in the shape of a large doughnut tapped Tansy on the shoulder. 'You shouldn't be here.'

'I . . . we . . . he . . .' stammered Tansy.

'West Green Academy,' Scott said, beaming. 'Our head arranged it with Patrick Goodlove – we're interviewing him for a project.'

'I do beg your pardon,' the woman beamed. 'He's about to speak but then we break for coffee. Catch him then.'

'Thanks, Scott, you were brilliant!' Tansy breathed. 'Wasn't he, Jade?'

'Mmm,' muttered Jade.

10.30 a.m.

Suffering to be beautiful

'How much longer?' Cleo demanded, fingering one of the strands of lotion coated hair sticking out of her plastic cap.

'About ten minutes,' Holly told her, glancing at her watch. 'How about I make a start on your eyebrows while we wait?'

'Do you have to?' Cleo winced.

'Definitely,' Holly replied, brandishing the tweezers. 'Get these shaped and you'll look totally different.'

'But I hate . . .'

'Close your eyes and shut up,' Holly said, laughing.

10.35 a.m.

'The secret with this product is to hit them hard . . . all about image . . . addictive taste . . . three for the price of two . . . big advertising campaign on British TV . . .'

Tansy leaned forward in her seat, her eyes glued on Pongo. He was thinner than he appeared in the photographs, which was cool. Her mum always said that Tansy could eat for England and never put on an ounce. She must have inherited that from him.

'Any questions?' Pongo had paused in his marketing spiel and was glancing around the auditorium. A few hands went up.

'As YummyScrum's marketing rep for the south-east, can you tell me how we should answer our critics?' asked a thin man in glasses. 'The ones who say that YummyScrum products are junk food with no nutritional value?'

'You tell 'em it straight,' drawled Pongo. 'You say that we've cut the fat content by twelve per cent and dramatically reduced the number of additives in the new recipe.'

'But that still means there's more fat in our product than our competitors, and we still pack in a fair whack of additives,' protested the questioner.

'That,' replied Pongo sharply, 'is not the kind of comment I expect to hear from anyone looking for promotion.'

10.41 a.m.

At The Cedars. Still in the bathroom and still struggling

'Ouch!' squealed Cleo.

'Sit still,' Holly ordered Cleo. 'If you want to look a million dollars for Jade's party you have to suffer a bit.'

'I wish Trig was still over here.' Cleo sighed. 'I hate going to parties and being the only one without a guy to snog.'

'You could have Scott,' Holly suggested. 'Jade doesn't seem to want him and he's quite cute.'

'I thought you still had a thing about him,' Cleo queried.

'I did,' admitted Holly. 'But I've matured. There's this guy, Kyle . . .'

10.43 a.m.

Why can't parents know their place?

Holly was yanking hairs out of Cleo's eyebrows and discussing pulling tactics when the front door slammed.

'Holly! It's Mum!'

Holly dropped the tweezers in dismay. 'I don't believe it,' she gasped. 'We're supposed to be doing homework. She'll go ballistic.'

'Where are you going?' Cleo gasped as Holly opened the bathroom door.

'To put her off the scent,' Holly told her.

'But the time is nearly up on my hair,' Cleo said. 'What do I do?'

'Just stay there,' Holly mouthed. 'Won't be a minute.'

She ran down the stairs. 'Hi, Mum,' she called 'What are you doing back so early? I thought – oh.'

She stopped in mid-sentence. Standing beside her mother was a somewhat overweight man in an ill-fitting suit, clutching a clipboard and peering at her over rimless glasses.

'This is Mr Rodhouse from the estate agent's,' her mother announced. 'He's come to value the house. This is my daughter, Holly.'

'Hi,' Holly said with a gulp. 'Does Dad . . .'

'So,' Mrs Vine butted in, glaring at Holly, 'where do you want to start? Upstairs?'

'No!' Holly gasped. 'I mean, Cleo and I are working and . . .'

'I'm pleased to hear it,' her mother replied.

'Don't worry, I'll start down here,' Mr Rodhouse announced, 'and make my own way upstairs in due course.'

'Fine.' Angela smiled. 'Coffee?'

10.44 a.m.
Emergency measures

'Cleo, quickly,' Holly urged, glancing anxiously at the mess in the bathroom. 'Shove all this stuff in the laundry basket and get into my room, like now.'

'But I'm about to rinse off . . .'

'It'll have wait,' Holly said. 'Wrap a towel round your head and if Mum comes . . .'

'It will all go wrong – the box said leave it on for fifteen minutes.'

'It said fifteen to twenty minutes,' Holly gabbled shoving the packaging into the laundry basket. 'And believe me, things will go a lot more wrong if my mother finds out what we've been doing.'

11.00 a.m.

Close encounters

'Hi, Patrick – remember me?' Scott strode up to Pongo, who was chatting to two earnest looking younger men. 'Scott Hamill – Trig's mate.'

'Well, hi there, Scottie!' drawled Pongo, slapping him on the back. 'What in the name of goodness are you doing here?'

'It's a school project,' Scott said, grabbing Tansy's wrist and shoving her forward. 'All about entrepreneurial skills for the twenty-first century. This is Tansy and she wants to interview you.'

'Hi.' Tansy's voice was a mere croak, partly because of fear and partly because her eyes were glued to his tie, which was patterned with lurid pink doughnuts.

'School project?' Pongo frowned, hardly glancing at her. 'I don't have time for all that kind of stuff right now, Scottie – deals to strike, money to make . . .'

Tansy's stomach flew into her mouth and for one awful moment she thought she would throw up right there on the paisley-patterned carpet.

'That's what our head said would happen,' Scott said,

sighing. 'YummyScrum aren't the kind of company to care about anything but making money, he said.'

Tansy and Jade exchanged glances. This was a side of Scott that they'd never seen before.

'Now, that is in no way true, but I'm a busy man . . .'

'Of course, I told him that I knew you weren't that kind of guy' said Scott. 'Guess I was wrong, though.'

'I hardly think the views of a load of schoolmasters need worry me too much.' Pongo laughed, nudging the guy on his left who obediently joined in with the laughter.

'I really need to talk to you,' Tansy cut in, suddenly finding her voice. 'It won't take long. I promise.'

'It might,' murmured another of the guys hovering at his side, 'make a good bit of publicity. You know, high flying exec of world-famous company takes time out to support youngsters . . . that sort of thing.'

Pongo's expression changed. 'Now you're talking,' he murmured. 'OK – you get ten minutes in here at twelve-thirty, OK?'

'Thank you, thank you,' Tansy began, but Pongo had already turned away.

'Make damn sure you get some good shots of me,' she heard him ordering his colleagues. 'You're right, we might be able to capitalise on this. And if I'm going to waste my time on kids, I want to be damn sure there's something worthwhile in it for YummyScrum.'

11.05 a.m.
Small adjustments

'All clear!' Holly hissed at Cleo. 'They're in the bedroom. Scoot downstairs to the downstairs loo and I'll rinse you off there. Oh . . .'

'What?' demanded Cleo.

'Nothing,' said Holly. 'I just need to balance your eyebrows up a bit. It'll be fine. Trust me.'

11.15 a.m.

'My goodness, what's that?' Holly's mother gasped as an air-piercing shriek resounded through the house.

'Sounds as if someone is being murdered in your kitchen,' the estate agent said and grinned. 'Don't worry about me – you go and check it out. I've got a lot more to do up here.'

Holly's mother ran down the stairs and pushed open the kitchen door. 'Holly? Cleo? What on earth is going on? Cleo – what on earth have you done to your hair?'

11.28 a.m.
Splitting hairs

'It wasn't my fault,' Holly protested, eyeing the green splodges all over Cleo's scalp and the rather tinny streaks in her hair. 'The packet said . . .'

'Cardboard can't speak,' her mother interjected,

clearly feeling that the correct use of English was more important than any beauty crisis.

'The instructions said,' said Holly with a sigh, 'that we had to leave it on for fifteen to twenty minutes.'

'Yes,' wailed Cleo, tears running down her cheeks. 'And you left it on for more than half an hour because your mum came back.'

'You are capable of rinsing it off yourself,' retorted Holly.

'You told me to hide,' sobbed Cleo. 'You said your mum would go ballistic.'

'Dead right,' snapped Mrs Vine. 'Holly, you said that Cleo was coming to help you with homework.'

'She is,' snapped Holly. 'She just wanted me to do her hair first.' She sighed. 'There is one good thing, Cleo,' she ventured. 'The TV people aren't likely to want you now. "Ordinary" you do not look.'

11.35 a.m.
To-dos about hairdos

'Cleo, do stop howling,' Mrs Vine said, sighing. 'A hairdresser will be able to put that right, no problem.'

'It's going to cost me a fortune.' Cleo sniffed.

'Wrong,' corrected Mrs Vine. 'It's going to cost Holly a fortune.' She paused and eyed Cleo. 'Are your eyebrows meant to look like that?'

12.20 p.m.

At Staverton Lakes. Feeling nervous

'It's nearly half-past twelve,' Jade told Tansy. 'You'd better get going.'

Tansy swallowed hard. 'This is it,' she murmured.

'Just remember it's your one and only chance and go for it,' Scott advised. 'See you later!'

12.25 p.m.

Back at The Cedars. Rescue mission.

'Right, Cleo, first things first,' Holly's mother declared. 'Eyebrows.'

'Holly did them,' Cleo said.

'I can see that.' Angela smiled. 'She's made you look permanently surprised. Give me the tweezers and sit still.'

12.30 p.m.

Taking the plunge

'Hello, Pongo.'

Patrick's mouth dropped open and his outstretched hand fell abruptly to his side. 'What did you call me?'

'Pongo,' stammered Tansy. 'That's your nickname, right?'

'Who told you that?' he demanded, gesturing for her to sit down in one of the red leather chairs.

For a second, Tansy felt as if her tongue was stuck to the roof of her mouth with fear. He hadn't denied it. It was him. She swallowed hard.

'Clarity told me. Clarity Meadows.'

'Clarity? Clarity?' He frowned. 'That name sounds familiar. Is she one of our Human Resources people?'

'No, she's my mum,' Tansy replied. 'And I'm Tansy.'

'Pretty name,' he commented, glancing at his watch. 'The photographer should be here any minute . . .'

'I was named after Tansy Fields near Glastonbury.'

'Glastonbury? Tansy Fields.' Pongo's eyes narrowed and he paled visibly. 'Clarity?'

Tansy could almost see his mind whirring back in time.

'What are you saying?' His voice had taken on a hard edge as he stared at her.

'I think – no, I'm certain – I'm your daughter,' she whispered, her voice wavering.

For a long moment, he said nothing. His hand gripped the arm of the chair and his eyes scanned her from head to foot.

At last he spoke. 'It's not possible,' he murmured, shaking his head. 'You can't be.'

'Look!' Tansy pulled the photo of Pongo, fifteen years earlier, from her pocket and handed it to him. He stared at it as colour flooded his cheeks.

'My God! Did your mom put you up to this?'

'She doesn't even know I'm here,' Tansy protested.

'But I can phone her and . . .'

She paused as a couple of press photographers appeared. '*Dunchester Mercury*,' said one. 'Come to take . . .'

'Not now,' Pongo interjected, waving them away. 'Give us five minutes, OK?'

The guys sniffed, glanced at their watches and shuffled off.

Pongo turned to Tansy. 'Look, I'm not sure what's going on here. Are you tell me that your mom is saying I'm your father? Just because we met years ago? What's she trying to do? Is it money? Is that it?'

'No!' Tansy shouted. 'She doesn't even like talking about you. For years, I didn't know who my dad was. I was the one who nagged and pushed to find out. Maybe I shouldn't have bothered.'

'Don't say that.' Pongo's face had softened. 'Look, maybe . . .'

'Patrick, you're needed urgently!' An officious looking woman, waving a clipboard, dashed across the room. 'Radio 4 – *Business Today* – on the line from London . . .'

Pongo stood up and nodded. 'Two minutes,' he told the woman, and then turned back to face Tansy. 'Look, this is mighty complicated,' he told her. 'I'll tell you straight – I don't believe I'm your dad. But . . .' He hesitated. 'How about you hang around for an hour or so, and we'll talk some more, OK?'

'You promise?'

'I promise. Look – take this pass, and meet me back here at one-thirty.'

12.40 p.m.
Manic mother

'But why did you do it?' Holly's mum asked. 'You've got lovely hair – why ruin it?'

'She didn't want to go on TV and if she looked normal, she would,' Holly said.

Her mother sighed. 'Could you translate that into basic English?' she asked. 'I don't – oh, hang on. Telephone.'

She grabbed the handset. 'Hello? Angela Vine here. What? Really? Oh wonderful!' She did a little skip of joy round the kitchen while Cleo and Holly looked on in amazement. 'What? No – I'll speak to my husband and get back to you. And thank you, thank you!' She threw the handset on to the worktop and punched the air. 'Yes, yes, YES!' she cried.

'Mum,' asked Holly patiently. 'What's going on?'

'That was the estate agent,' Mrs Vine enthused. 'He says this house is very saleable and what's more, he's got a client looking for just this sort of thing. A guy who wants to do it up and convert it into flats.'

'But Dad said . . .'

'Look, love,' her mum explained. 'I know Dad loves this place but he's getting older and the house needs such a lot of work. I want us to have a smaller place, somewhere we can enjoy retirement.'

'He'll never agree,' Holly warned her.

'We'll see,' her mother said, smiling.

12.50 p.m.
Mum'll fix it

'I'm sorry, Cleo,' Holly said for the fifth time. 'Really, I am.'

'It's not your fault,' Cleo acknowledged. 'It was a dumb idea anyway. Thinking I could ever look anything but a total dweeb.'

'Stop that right now!' Holly's mother interrupted, dumping a plate of cheese and tomato sandwiches on the kitchen table. 'I didn't ask you to stop for lunch in order to hear you criticising yourself all the time.'

She eased herself on to one of the kitchen chairs and grabbed a sandwich. 'Right,' she went on. 'This is the plan. I've telephoned your mother . . .'

'You haven't?' Holly gasped. 'Mum, that was the dumbest thing you could . . .'

'. . . to tell her that Cleo is spending the day here,' she finished, glaring at Holly. 'I've arranged for my hairdresser to fit you in at two-thirty, Cleo. While you're there, I'll prepare Diana for the shock.'

'Thanks,' Cleo murmured.

'I thought, perhaps, that one of those bedpost haircuts might do the trick.'

Cleo and Holly burst out laughing.

'What? What have I said?'

'Bedhead, Mum,' spluttered Holly.

'Whatever,' said her mother. 'At least Cleo's smiling again.'

1.30 p.m.

Tansy glanced round the delegates' refreshment room. Clusters of people were munching on sandwiches and waitresses were circulating with drinks on trays. There was no sign of Pongo. He'll come in a minute, she assured herself. He promised.

'Excuse me, honey.' A vast woman in a pair of orange and black checked trousers and a fluffy sweater wobbled her way up to one of the waitresses as she passed Tansy's chair. 'Have you seen Mr Patrick Goodlove?'

'I wouldn't know him if I had,' replied the waitress in a bored voice.

'I'm waiting for him!' Tansy jumped to her feet. 'He said he'd be here by half-past one.'

'And you are?' the woman enquired, a slight frown puckering her brow.

'I'm Tansy Meadows,' she said. 'I'm his – well, I'm doing a school project and I'm waiting to interview him.'

'Now isn't that just darling?' the woman cooed, patting her immaculate flame-coloured hair. 'That is so neat of him to agree to help you along.' She grinned. 'I have to say he's not always that accommodating!'

'Do you work with him?' Tansy asked, hoping to glean a bit more information before he arrived.

'Work? Oh my goodness no, honey. I'm Felicity Goodlove. I'm Patrick's wife.'

1.52 p.m.

Wife. Wife. Tansy repeated the word in her head. He's married, she thought miserably. He and mum won't be getting together again. What's more, will this woman want me within a mile of Pongo? Well, there's only one way to find out. She took a deep breath and bit her lip.

1.53 p.m.
Shock, horror

'Say, honey, are you all right?' Felicity peered anxiously at Tansy.

'You've gone a very funny colour.'

'I'm fine,' she began. 'I'd better go . . .'

'Go? No way!' cried Felicity. 'Patrick will be here directly. He may not be hot on punctuality but he always – talk of the devil! Here he comes now!'

Tansy looked up. Pongo had stopped dead in his tracks. He looked first at Tansy, then at his wife, then back to Tansy. And instantly, Tansy knew what he was thinking.

'Mr Goodlove,' Tansy said, trying to keep the tremor out of her voice, 'how good of you to come! I've just been telling your wife about my school project.' She paused, noticing the way he was clenching and unclenching his fists. 'That's all we've had time to talk about,' she added holding his gaze.

He shook himself slightly and found his voice. 'Great,' he said. 'Well, Felicity, honey, if you just pop downstairs and make yourself beautiful, I'll give this young lady a couple of minutes and then you and me will hit the shops.'

'Brush the dust off the credit cards, loverboy!' Felicity gave him an affectionate punch. 'Good to have met you, Tansy. Be gentle with her, Patrick. Bye now!'

1.55 p.m.

It was like this . . .

'And you didn't say a word about this crazy idea?' Pongo slumped into a chair and beckoned to a waitress. 'Coffee, black, no sugar,' he ordered.

'Please,' muttered the waitress under her breath before stomping off across the room.

'It's not crazy,' Tansy asserted. 'And no, I didn't mention it. I'm not that insensitive.'

'Appreciate that,' Pongo replied. 'Look, I guess it's time I came clean. I do remember Clarity. Very well.'

Tansy's heart soared.

'She was a beautiful girl - not unlike you,' he said. 'Plumper, though. We had a ball that summer - a whole crowd of us. But we were just kids.'

'Kids can have babies,' Tansy reminded him.

'I know that.' He nodded. 'But we didn't. Trust me, you are not mine.'

The nausea that had been hovering in Tansy's stomach all morning came back with a vengeance. 'How can you be so sure?'

Patrick inspected his fingernails and glanced over his shoulder to check that no one was eavesdropping.

'Look,' he said, so quietly that Tansy had to lean forward to catch his words, 'what I'm about to tell – it's not easy.'

'Go on.'

'Felicity and I have been trying for years to have children.' He sighed. 'Frankly, I'm not bothered either way, but she's desperate. There's nothing wrong with her, and I've always made out it was my fault. If she thought I'd got a kid . . .'

'So you admit it's a possibility?'

Pongo looked at her long and hard. 'Damn it – I don't know!' He thumped his fist on the arm of the chair. 'No – yes – it's possible.'

Suddenly, he didn't look like the over-confident businessman. He looked confused and lost and scared.

'It's OK,' she said. 'I'm not going to tell your wife. I just needed to meet you, that's all.'

'And now that you have?' he demanded, avoiding her gaze.

'I guess that's up to you,' she said.

'You're a decent kid, you know that?' He stood up, hands stuffed into his trousers pockets. 'But too much has happened since then – you can't turn the clock back . . .'

'But you could have done!' Tansy burst out. 'Why didn't you answer Mum's letters?'

'What letters?'

'The ones telling you about me – she wrote loads of times . . .'

'I never got a letter,' Pongo protested.

'Oh, like you really expect me to believe that!' Tansy's fury amazed even her. 'One letter might go astray – but five?'

'Honest to God, I swear I never got them. If I had . . .'

'If you had? Would things have been different?'

He shrugged his shoulders. 'Who knows? It's not important now.'

Tansy's eyes filled with tears. 'Oh, right? So that's it, is it? I'm unimportant, I'm no one . . .'

'Tansy, stop it,' Patrick whispered urgently. 'Please. Now.' His face was turning paler by the second, but Tansy no longer cared.

'No, I won't stop it,' she cried. 'Do you know what you're saying?'

'Really, I've given up precious time to give you this interview and . . .'

'And now you're bored, right? Too bored to spare another single second for your own daughter! Well, stuff you!'

She spun round on her heel to storm out of the room. And saw at once just why Pongo had looked so sick. Felicity was standing three feet away, staring at them mouth in open-mouthed horror. Tansy's anger turned to guilt and she did the only thing she could. She ran.

2.45 p.m.
At the hairdresser's. Hoping

'What we will do,' announced the hairdresser, fingering Cleo's green-streaked hair and examining her dyed scalp, 'is cut all this out, make it really short and funky, then give it a remedial treatment, bring the colour back . . .'

'How much,' Holly said with a gulp, 'will all that cost?'

'Forty-five pounds should do it,' the hairdresser replied.

Holly gulped again.

'Call it thirty-five.' The hairdresser smiled. 'Accidents happen to the best of us.'

2.55 p.m.
Telling Cleo's mum the horrid truth

'Angela! What a surprise!' Mrs Greenway flung open the front door and beckoned Holly's mum inside. 'It's so good to see you.'

'You might not think that,' said Mrs Vine, sighing, 'when you hear what I've got to tell you.'

3.00 p.m.

'Don't cry,' Jade pleaded, handing Tansy a tissue. Scott was hovering in the background, looking everywhere but at Tansy's distraught face.

'I've been such a fool,' Tansy sobbed. 'And now his wife will be in a state, and it's all my fault.'

'Come on,' Jade said in one last attempt to cheer her up. 'What's it to be? Ice cream or doughnuts?'

'Neither,' sniffed Tansy. 'I just want to go home.'

3.20 p.m.

She did all that to avoid being on the show?' Mrs Greenway looked aghast as Holly's mother told her the saga of Cleo's makeover efforts. 'The child must be off her head – it'll be the greatest fun.'

'For you, maybe,' said Mrs Vine sternly. 'Not for Cleo. She thinks the only reason she was needed for the show was because she looks like a – what's the word they use?'

'Dweeb?' offered Cleo's mum.

'That's the one,' Holly's mum agreed. 'What is a dweeb, exactly?'

3.45 p.m.
Mopping-up operations

'Oh there you are!' Tansy's mother cried as her daughter slammed the front door. 'I'm glad you're here because . . . darling, what is it? What on earth has happened?'

Tansy flung herself into her mother's arms and sobbed. 'I'm sorry – I wouldn't have – only it seemed too good to be true and then when he didn't want . . .'

'Stop right there,' her mum said, taking her hand and leading her into the sitting room. 'Now sit down, take a deep breath and start at the very beginning.'

3.50 p.m.
Regrets

'I kind of hoped there'd be a happy ending.' Jade sighed as she walked to the corner of the road with Scott.

'I guess they don't often happen,' grunted Scott. 'Like – well, you and me. You don't want to get back with me, do you?'

Jade took a deep breath. 'I really like you, Scott,' she said. 'You're a great mate. But . . .'

'Go on, say it.'

'It was just all the heavy stuff that I couldn't hack,' she admitted. 'You wanted to spend minute of every day with me – I felt suffocated.'

Scott kicked at a piece of cardboard blowing down the pavement in the wind. 'Great – so I'm on my own, right?'

'You don't need to be.' Jade grinned. 'Not when you've got girls drooling for you.'

'Oh sure,' Scott muttered. 'Like who?'

4.00 p.m.
Back home at Kestrel Close

'You've been out all day!' Allegra cried as Jade walked through the door. 'What have you been doing?'

'Sorting out your love life,' remarked Jade. 'Now it's up to you.'

4.18 p.m.
Getting through another box of tissues

'Are you very angry?' Tansy sniffed, wiping her eyes on a crumpled tissue.

'With you? No darling,' her mother replied. 'With Pongo – bloody furious! OK, so I've known for ages he was your dad, and I've come to terms with the fact that he ignored us both – but to hurt you like that . . . Just you wait till I get my hands on him!'

'You can't say anything,' Tansy protested. 'His wife . . .'

'His *wife*?' For an instant, her mum's face clouded. 'What about her?'

'It's a long story,' sighed Tansy.

4.25 p.m.

Keep calm, Tansy's mother told herself as Tansy poured out the rest of her story. You're the parent here. Just because Pongo is in the same town doesn't give you the right to turn to jelly and act like a lovesick teenager. You did that once before and look what happened.

'I don't get it,' she murmured. 'How can Pongo work for a company like YummyScrum? They only make junk food and he used to be so fussy about what he ate. I used to cook for him over the campfire and . . .'

That, thought Tansy, is probably what put him on to burgers and chips. Nettle soup can get very boring after a while.

'Mum, you're crying!' she gasped, suddenly catching sight of her mother's face. 'It's my fault, isn't it? I should never have gone.'

She shook her head. 'Of course you should, darling,' she replied. 'I was just thinking about the past, that's all. And kicking myself for being such an idiot.'

'Hey,' said Tansy, giving her a hug and trying to be brave. 'You weren't an idiot. You got me. That showed great taste!'

Her mother grinned. 'Let's have toasted teacakes and blueberry muffins,' she said. 'I'll nip out and get some.'

'They're junk food,' Tansy said teasingly. 'You don't approve of junk food.'

'Today I do,' said Clarity, grinning. 'There are times when only junk will do.'

5.00 p.m.
At the hairdresser's

'That looks – well, amazing,' Holly exclaimed, as the stylist worked styling cream through Cleo's freshly-cropped hair. 'Very trendy.'

Cleo stared at her reflection. The bronze and silver highlights were now only a few centimetres long and her fringe had totally disappeared.

'I don't look like me any more,' she said, groaning.

'I thought,' remarked Holly, 'that was the general idea.'

6.00 p.m.
The Cedars. Breaking the news . . .

'Rupert, dear,' said Holly's mother, the moment her husband walked in through the door. 'I've found out all about The Laurels.'

'So tell me the worst.'

'Well, dear, it's going to become a day nursery. Up to thirty children, they reckon, once the conversion is complete and the garden turned into a playground. Be lovely to hear the sound of little voices all day, won't it?'

7.00 p.m.
And stirring the pot . . .

'I was thinking, Rupert dear, that we could offer people cut price car parking in our front drive – the street will be so crowded morning and evening with parents dropping off and fetching . . .'

7.30 p.m.
And going in for the kill . . .

'Would you credit it, Rupert dear? I happened to be chatting to a guy from the estate agent's today and they said we could get at least £375,000 for this place. Of course, I said it wasn't up for sale and he said what a pity, because he had a client desperate to buy something of this sort . . .'

9.00 p.m.
Result!

'What are you doing, Rupert? Oh – are those the property pages of the *Telegraph*? No, of course, you're just browsing. Good idea. Keep your finger on the pulse, that's what you always say, isn't it? Gin and tonic, dear?

9.20 p.m
Financial matters

'Mum,' Holly began. 'You know I had to take all that money out of my bank account to sort Cleo's hair? Well, now I can't afford a present for Jade and I'll look a real meanie.'

'My purse is on the kitchen table – take a ten-pound note and don't ever mess with cheap hair dye again,' her mother sighed.

'I won't, I promise. I've learned my lesson,' Holly assured her.

'If I believed that, I'd believe anything.' Her mother grinned. 'Now, about that homework – your father's going to help you.'

'In a minute,' Mr Vine muttered, without taking his eyes off the newspaper. 'I'm a little tied up right now.'

FRIDAY

1.00 a.m.

3 Plough Cottages. Tossing . . .

She knew she should never have done it, never said all that stuff to Pongo. She'd blown it. She was a fool.

3.15 a.m.

. . . and turning

And what if her mum had got it all wrong? What if it was that other guy she hung around with that summer? She had heard all about Jordan, the other boyfriend from that summer way back – the one who spent his time painting pebbles. A pebble-painting father wasn't quite what she had in mind. Maybe, she thought, life was easier without a father.

7.45 a.m.

Reprieved

'Wake up, you've overslept! It's a quarter to eight and you'll be late for school.'

Tansy felt her shoulder being shaken. She groaned and turned over.

'Tansy, come on darling – wake up!'

'I can't,' she groaned. 'I've been awake half the night.'

Her mother perched on the edge of the bed. 'Bad dreams?' she asked, stroking Tansy's tousled hair. 'About yesterday? Me, too.'

Tansy struggled to sit up and pulled the duvet up to her chin. 'Mum, what if they split up?' she gabbled. 'Pongo and his wife? Because of me blurting out about being his kid? What if I'm a home-breaker? What if . . .'

'Darling, I know you got an A* for drama last term, but I think you're getting things a bit skewed.'

'But we don't know, do we?' Tansy persisted. 'I mean, I just ran off and left them to it. I should have explained . . .' She paused to yawn. 'I'm so tired,' she moaned. 'Do I have to go to school?'

'No.'

'Please don't make me – what did you say?'

'I said,' repeated her mother, 'that you don't have to go to school. Because there is something far more important that you and I have to do today.'

'What?'

'Go back to sleep. I'll tell you later.'

8.10 a.m.
Off the hook

'Cleo, give this cash to Holly when you get to school,' her mother told her, handing her an envelope. 'It's the money for sorting your hair.'

'Her mum said she had to pay it . . .'

'I know.' Her mother sighed. 'But as Angela pointed out, it's all my fault you felt you had to change, anyway.'

Cleo looked at her mother. She had dark lines under her eyes and looked much older than usual. 'I'm sorry it all went wrong,' Cleo murmured. 'I just wanted to . . .'

'Get out of the TV show,' her mother finished. 'I know. I was wrong to force it on you. Still, they weren't that bothered when I cancelled.'

'You cancelled?' Cleo gasped. 'But you need the money.'

Her mum nodded. 'Tell me about it. But there will be other jobs – and your feelings matter more.'

'I do love you, Mum,' Cleo said giving her mother a hug. 'I'm sorry I'm so boring.'

'Cleopatra Desdemona Greenway,' retorted her mother, pulling back and glaring at her, 'if I hear you putting yourself down one more time, I shall sign you up for one of those shows where they give you a personality makeover. Now repeat after me, "I am one great kid."'

9.00 a.m.
In registration

'Tansy Meadows?' Mr Grubb paused and looked up from his register. 'Anyone know what's happened to Tansy?'

'She's got problems, Sir,' Scott called out.

'Nice one, Scott,' said Jade, sighing. 'Tell the world, why don't you?'

9.30 a.m.
At home in bed

Tansy yawned and grabbed her mobile as it bleeped on her bedside table.

'VOICEMAIL,' she read and punched the button.

'Hi Tansy, it's Holly. Look, I'm just leaving a message to say I'm here if you need me. OK, so I'm miffed you didn't tell me about your dad and all, but I guess you had your reasons. Oh, and when you see Cleo, tell her that her hair looks great. Even you have to lie a little. Talk soon, loads of love. Bye!'

10.15 a.m.
At school, wishing she was home in bed

'If one more person says to me, "Oh, Cleo, what have you done to your hair?" I won't be responsible for my actions,' Cleo growled as she and Holly put on overalls in the science lab. 'I'm going to look a right mess at the party.'

'No you're not,' Holly assured her. 'Let me do your make-up and . . .'

'No, thanks,' Cleo cut in. 'I'll be fine. I'll borrow a hat.'

12.30 p.m.
Searching for sustenance

'Feeling better?' her mother asked as Tansy appeared in the kitchen, wrapped in her bathrobe. 'Ready for some lunch?'

'What is it?' Tansy asked.

'Pizza,' said her mother.

'You mean, normal, regular pizza? No seaweed? No stinging nettles?'

Her mother laughed. 'You don't put that stuff on pizzas.'

'When you cook, Mum, one can never be too sure.'

12.45 p.m.
In the school cafeteria

'Jade, what time's the party tomorrow?' Brooke asked, queuing behind Jade at the drinks machine.

'Eight till eleven,' Jade said. 'We've got a disco coming to the house and everything. Should be cool.'

'It'll be a right rave,' Brooke said, grinning. 'Me and my mates can't wait.'

12.55 p.m.
Tansy's house

'So that's my plan,' Tansy's mother concluded, wiping her mouth on her table napkin. 'What do you think?'

'I think it's brilliant,' Tansy told her. 'But are you sure you want to?'

'I've never been more sure of anything,' her mother replied. 'Now go and get dressed.'

3.00 p.m.
Success!

'Rupert, what on earth are you doing home at this hour?' gasped Mrs Vine. 'It's not half day at the museum – are you ill?' She looked at him anxiously.

'No, I'm fine,' he assured her. 'I've been thinking about this house. Now hear me out before you protest.'

'Right, dear.'

'It occurs to me,' her husband said, 'having thought it all through very carefully, that it might be a good time to think about selling.'

'Do you think so, darling?' she replied, trying to stifle her glee. 'Well, if that's what you think is best . . .'

'I do,' he nodded. 'I'm going to the estate agent right now. And don't try talking me out of it.'

'I wouldn't dream of it, dear,' his wife said, and smiled.

4.00 p.m
Friends

'Hi, I missed you so I thought I'd drop by on my way home!' Jade gave Tansy a hug, and dumped her school bag on the hall floor.

'Cool,' grinned Tansy. 'Want a drink?'

Jade shook her head. 'No thanks,' she replied. 'I told Scott I didn't want to be his girlfriend.'

'I thought you'd done that already.' Tansy frowned.

'I had,' said Jade, sighing. 'But this time I think he believes me.'

'And you're having second thoughts, right?' Tansy added.

'No way,' Jade said.

'So is there someone else?' Tansy persisted.

Why, thought Jade, does everyone think you have to have a guy in tow? 'There might be,' she said with a smile. That would shut Tansy up for a bit. Hopefully.

5.30 p.m.

Motherly support

'Mum, are you sure you want to do this?' Tansy asked as her mother pulled up outside Staverton Lakes Hotel.

'Yes,' her mother replied shortly. 'You're right – it's unfinished business and for everyone's sake, we have to deal with it.' She swallowed hard and squeezed Tansy's hand. 'That's not to say,' she admitted, 'that I'm not as nervous as hell.'

She marched up to the Reception Desk. 'I'm looking for Pong – I mean, Patrick Goodlove,' she said.

'Mr Goodlove?' the hotel concierge queried. 'He should be coming out of the meeting right now. The Madison Suite – down the corridor, second left. Shall I ring through to say . . .'

'No, thank you.' Tansy's mother smiled. 'It's a surprise.'

5.36 p.m.

'Oh no!' Tansy stood stock still and grabbed her mother's arm. 'That's her – Felicity – his wife!' She gestured to a woman standing outside the Madison Suite, impatiently tapping her foot and glancing at her diamond-encrusted watch.

'Mum, we can't – we . . .'

At that moment, the woman looked up and caught Tansy's eye. 'Well, hello there. It's Tammy, isn't it?' Felicity called, waddling towards them.

'Tansy,' said Tansy.

'I'm Tansy's mum. Clarity Meadows. And please, believe me, we haven't come to make trouble. We just want to explain things and then we'll . . .'

'Well, isn't this just the loveliest thing?' enthused Felicity. 'And look, here comes Patrick!'

She waved vigorously as the doors opened and Pongo appeared, black briefcase in hand and a weary expression on his face. 'Patrick, cherub. Look who's here!' she called.

Tansy cringed in embarrassment as several delegates turned their heads to stare in her direction. 'Now come on, let's go into the lounge and have some of your wonderful English afternoon tea.'

Felicity beamed at her speechless guests and turned to the open-mouthed Pongo. 'For heaven's sake, dear, don't just stand there. Get your daughter a drink and some cookies.'

6.50 p.m.
In full flood

'. . . and we have a lovely apartment in Chicago, a little holiday ranch in Montana, just near to Great Falls and then the darlingest beach house on Cape Cod. Ah, there you are, Patrick dear – I was just telling Tansy and Charity . . .'

'Clarity . . .' Tansy's mum interjected when Felicity finally paused for breath.

'Sorry dear, Clarity – all about our homes. Tansy must come visit, mustn't she? You can get to know one another and she and I can do girlie things together. It'll be a blast!'

'Felicity, stop it!' Pongo gave up attempting to chew on a scone and pushed his plate away. 'This is not appropriate!' He turned slowly to face Tansy's mother and his eyes scanned her from head to foot. 'You've changed.'

'Motherhood does that to people,' she said curtly. 'Look, we probably shouldn't have come, but . . .'

'It was my fault,' Tansy cut in. 'I wanted to make sure that you two hadn't fallen out because of what I said. I mean, it's not like Pongo . . .'

'Fallen out? On the contrary, I couldn't be happier!' Felicity clapped her chubby hands together, and her gold bangles jangled on her wrists.

'You don't mind?'

'If you are Pongo's daughter,' Felicity said, suddenly serious, 'then I can start hoping all over again.'

'Hoping?' Tansy's mother frowned.

'That we can have a kid of our own,' Felicity said, colouring slightly. 'If he can manage it once . . .'

'Felicity, for heaven's sake . . .' Pongo hissed.

'But aren't you too old?' Tansy butted in and then winced at her own tactlessness.

'I'm only forty-one,' Felicity said. 'Plenty of time yet. Isn't there, Patrick darling?'

6.55 p.m.
Enough is enough

'So there we are,' Felicity declared, handing Tansy a card. 'All our phone numbers and addresses so you be sure to keep in touch now.'

'We must go,' her mother cut in. 'Thank you for the tea. Tansy, come along. Now.' She stood up, brushed some cake crumbs from her lap and walked briskly out into the corridor followed by Tansy.

'Clarity, wait.'

Pongo chased after them down the corridor as they made their way to the lift. 'Look, I'm sorry about Felicity . . .'

'Don't be,' she said, her voice still strained. 'I think she took it very well.'

'I didn't mean that,' Pongo explained. 'She gets a bit over the top, makes all these invitations, wants to embrace the whole universe to her bosom.' He gave a nervous laugh.

'And you don't, is that it?' Tansy's mother rejoined.

'I don't know whether I'm Tansy's father or not,' he gabbled, his eyes looking everywhere but at the two of them. 'I guess there's DNA testing we could do . . .'

'No,' cut in Tansy. 'I don't want that. And you don't really want me, do you?'

'It's not like that,' Patrick objected. 'It's just that I have my life and my work and - well, all I came to say was that I'm sorry.'

'What for? Having me?'

Tansy's mother put a hand on Tansy's shoulder. 'Steady, love,' she said. 'I'm not sorry, Pongo - having Tansy has made my life a joy. It's just a shame you weren't around to share it . . .'

'Look, I'm a wealthy man - and even though I think this could be one huge mistake, I can send a cheque every few months . . .'

'No,' she said firmly. 'I'm sure you mean it very kindly, but we don't want your money. We have something that money can't buy.' She took a deep breath. 'Go home and be happy. As happy as I am. Please?'

Pongo looked at her long and hard and his hand brushed hers. 'Thank you,' he said. 'Thank you both.'

8.10 p.m.

Struggling with science

'Holly, it's quite simple,' her father sighed after an hour of trying to explain the basics of Key Stage Four science.

'Not to me, it isn't,' Holly replied. 'Dad, why can't I just drop double award and do single science? Or no science at all?'

'Holly, that's a defeatist attitude,' her father declared. 'The Vines don't give in. Now read page eleven again.'

8.15 p.m.
Comfort food

'Hot chocolate and marshmallows,' Holly's mum declared, after Rupert had stomped out of the room to answer the telephone. 'And don't worry, darling – I'll have a word with dad.'

'He said that the Vines don't give in,' muttered Holly.

'He said the Vines didn't move house,' her mother reminded her, 'and look at him now.'

9.30 p.m.
In Tansy's bedroom

'Goodnight, darling.' Tansy's mum gave her a hug and kissed the top of her head. 'Are you sure you're OK?'

Tansy nodded. 'I'm fine,' she said, smiling. 'Why wouldn't I be? I've got the best mum in the world.'

SATURDAY

8.30 a.m.
Birthday girl

'Happy birthday to you, happy birthday to you, happy birthday, dear Jade, happy birthday to you!'

Jade tried hard to smile at the whole family clustered round the breakfast table.

'I've got you this,' her little cousin Helen said, thrusting a parcel into Jade's hands. 'It's earrings.'

'You're not meant to tell her,' her mother laughed. 'And this is from us, dear.'

Oh Mum, Dad, Jade thought, as the presents piled up and everyone made a fuss of her. All I want is you two here. Now. Why did you have to die?

9.10 a.m.
Memories

'Jade?' Her uncle tapped on her door. 'May I come in?'

'Yes.' Jade hastily wiped her eyes with the back of her hand.

'Look,' he said, closing the door behind him. 'We both know what a difficult day this is for you, and I'm not here to say too much. But Paula and I thought you'd like this.' He pushed a small package into her hands.

'But you gave me the brilliant CD player,' she said.

'This is just something extra, something personal,' he said. 'We didn't want to give it to you in front of the others.' She ripped at the wrapping paper and opened a small black box. Lying on a bed of tissue was a pendant.

'The diamond is from your mum's engagement ring, and the gold is from your dad's signet ring,' he told her. 'And the chain . . .'

'. . . is the one Mum wore all the time,' Jade finished, her eyes filling with tears. 'It's beautiful, Uncle David. Thank you.'

She frowned. 'Where's Paula?'

'It's a tough day for her too,' he reminded her. 'Your mum was her sister, after all. Why don't you go and give her a hug?'

10.00 a.m.
Telling it like it is

'Tansy? Andy's here!'

Tansy threw her bathrobe round her shoulders and ran downstairs. Andy was standing in the hall, glasses crooked as usual, and he didn't look happy.

'So why didn't you tell me what was going on?' he demanded the moment Tansy's mum had retreated into the kitchen and shut the door. 'About meeting up with your dad and all that.'

'Who told you?' Tansy asked.

'Scott,' Andy replied shortly. 'I called him last night.'

'Why?'

'Why do you think?' Andy countered in disbelief. 'Because I was worried about you not being at school yesterday and Mum said she'd seen you talking to Scott in town.'

'I would have told you,' Tansy began.

'Would you?' Andy didn't sound convinced. 'This week you've really been shutting me out and I don't get it.'

Tansy pulled a face. 'I'm sorry,' she sighed. 'It's just that it all happened so fast, I was in such a muddle – it just seemed easier not to tell anyone.'

'Anyone except Scott and Jade and probably half the rest of the universe, for all I know,' Andy retorted. 'I thought we were a couple.'

'We are,' Tansy said, sighing. 'Well, sort of.'

'Oh, it's sort of now, is it?' Andy glared. 'Look, the other day when you asked about my mum, I said I was there for you. Then you go and cut me out completely. What's the problem?'

'Do you really want to know what was on my mind? Why I kept my distance?' Tansy demanded. 'Well, I'll tell you. The twins.'

Andy's anger changed to a look of pure astonishment. 'The twins? What have Clover and Baz got to do with anything?'

Tansy took a deep breath. 'No one knows who their dad is, either,' she reminded him gently. 'Except your mum, of course. One day they might want to do exactly what I did.'

'I hadn't thought of that,' Andy admitted. 'I guess I actually tried not to think of that.'

'I know what it's like to spend half your life wondering where you came from,' Tansy explained. 'I guessed it was hard for you to too, and I didn't know what to say to you but I would have told you when everything was sorted.'

'And is it sorted now?' Andy's tone was gentler.

Tansy gave a wry smile. 'Not exactly,' she said. 'It's hard to know where to start.'

'How about the beginning?' suggested Andy. 'I'm in no rush.'

10.30 a.m.

Not telling it at all

'I thought I'd just look in to see if everything was OK,' Kyle's mother said when Tansy's mother opened the front door. 'You said that you were having a crisis.'

'Sort of,' Tansy's mother said, ushering her into the kitchen. 'Honestly though, I sometimes wonder why we ever bothered with men.'

'Me too. Do you want to talk about it or shall I shut up?'

'No,' her mother said firmly. 'It's in the past. Let's talk about the future. Now I've drawn up a plan for the roof garden at Staverton. What I thought was this . . .'

11.30 a.m.

Party Planners Inc.

'It looks great, doesn't it?' Allegra surveyed the conservatory and sitting room bedecked with banners and balloons. 'Pity about the carpet – I wonder if we should roll it back.'

'You can wonder all you like,' her mother said, peering round the door. 'The answer is no.'

'In which case,' Jade cut in with a smile, 'we might as well go shopping.'

12.10 p.m.

'Kyle? It's Holly Vine here. Just checking about this evening. What time are you getting to Jade's place? Seven? Cool – see you then. Bye!'

She punched Tansy's number into her mobile phone. 'We're going shopping,' she declared. 'I'll be round in ten minutes. What? Of course you feel like it – it'll do you good. Besides I need your help in finding a stunning outfit with only £18.75 to spend.'

1.15 p.m.

Retail therapy . . .

'Too tight,' Allegra said to Jade. 'You won't be able to sit down.'

'So I stand up all evening,' Jade suggested.

'What – and miss a good sofa snog? Get real.'

'Not everyone is into snogging.' Jade sighed.

'You,' replied Allegra, 'are sadly strange.'

1.35 p.m.
. . . on a budget

'Too expensive.' Holly sighed, tossing a really sexy camitop back on the rack. 'This is hopeless.'

'Couldn't you get your mum to lend you the money?' Tansy suggested.

'Could you stop the earth rotating?'

'Got it!' cried Tansy. 'Charity shops!'

'What?' Holly shuddered. 'They're full of old people's clothes – pleated skirts and nasty little cardigans with bobbly bits.'

'No way,' Tansy said. 'Come on – this could be fun.'

At least she looks a bit more cheerful, thought Holly. Even if she has totally lost the plot.

2.15 p.m.
. . . and success

'You're sure?' Jade urged Allegra. 'It doesn't make my bum look too big?'

'No.'

'And the colour suits me?'

'Yes.'

'You're not just saying that?'

'*Jade!*'

'OK, OK, I'll get them.'

2.30 p.m.

Saved at the Save the Children Shop

'Wow!' Tansy stared at Holly. She was wearing gold satin trousers and a black chiffon crossover camisole with tiny sequins round the neck. 'You look amazing,' she said.

'Amazing as in terrific, or amazing as in oh-my-god-what's-she-wearing?' asked Holly.

'Just buy them, Holly,' said Tansy. 'I want to wash my hair.'

3.15 p.m.

Witnessing a small miracle

'Holly?' Tansy stopped dead outside Holly's house. 'You never said your house was for sale.'

'I didn't know it was,' gasped Holly, staring at the For Sale board which a man in a fluorescent jacket was hammering into the edge of the driveway. 'Mind you, I'm usually the last to know anything round here.'

She unlocked the front door and beckoned to Tansy to follow her. 'Mum?' she called. 'There's a man . . .'

'I know, isn't it wonderful!' Her mother burst out of

the kitchen, her cheeks flushed. 'And I don't know why you are so surprised.'

'Dad said . . .'

'I told you it would happen,' her mother interrupted smugly. 'And I'm very rarely wrong.'

6.55 p.m.

'Holly, take that stuff off your face now,' exploded Mr Vine. 'You are not going out looking like that.'

'What's wrong with it?'

'You want a list?'

7.00 p.m.

'Cleo, why are you wearing a hat?' Portia, her sister, asked.

'To cover up my hair,' replied Cleo.

'Not the way at all,' Portia announced, whipping it off her head. 'Make it a feature. Come upstairs, I'll sort you out.'

7.30 p.m.
Panic and pep talks

'Tansy, are you ready?' her mother called up the stairs.

Tansy sat on the bed in her bra and panties. It was no good. She wasn't in a party mood. 'I'm not going,' she called down the stairs. 'I can't face it.' She heard her mother pounding up the stairs.

'Now, we are not having any of that nonsense,' she declared. 'This is Jade's party right? Jade, your friend? Who lost both parents last year? Who's probably feeling pretty uptight herself, remembering what it used to be like?'

'It's just that what with Pongo . . .'

Her mother put her arm round Tansy's shoulders. 'Listen, sweetheart, you can't let things like that eat away at you. You've had a tough few days and I understand how you feel. But the bottom line is this – you have to take a deep breath, hold your head high and get on with life.'

'I suppose,' nodded Tansy. 'OK, I'll give it a go.'

7.30 p.m.
Lustful longings

Jade watched Kyle's muscles ripple as he her carried speakers into the house. He is pretty fit, she thought.

'This is Angus,' he said, catching her eye and jerking his head in the direction of an athletic looking guy with jet black spiked hair, who was trailing a jumble of leads behind him.

He dumped the speakers in the middle of the floor. 'OK, so where do you want us?' he asked.

'That would be telling,' she said with a grin. See, she told herself as Kyle threw back his head and laughed, I can do the chat up bit as well as anyone.

Pity my heart's not in it.

8.00 p.m.
Panicking parent

'Hi, Warren, hi, Ursula – gorgeous necklace – oh thanks, Tansy, that's really kind of you . . . love the shoes . . . Allegra, this is Alex . . .'

Jade was in the middle of welcoming her mates when her aunt came running down the stairs, clutch bag in one hand and a sheet of paper in the other.

'Now this is the address of the restaurant – it's only a mile or so away – and the doctor's phone number is on the pinboard. The pizzas are coming at nine-thirty, Josh is over the road at Adam's house if you need him and we'll be back by ten-thirty'

'Mum, stop fussing,' Allegra ordered her. 'This is a party, not the outbreak of world war. Everything's going to be fine.'

8.01 p.m.
Tetchy teen

'Where's Scott?' Allegra asked Jade anxiously. 'He should be here by now.'

'He is only one minute late,' Jade said, laughing. 'Give the guy a break.'

8.10 p.m.

Small talk . . .

'Hey, Cleo, your hair is stunning!' Tansy exclaimed, raising her voice over the beat of the disco. 'Really cool – it makes you look so . . . funky.'

'Straight up? I don't feel like me at all.'

'You don't look like you, either,' Tansy said. 'Those earrings and the flower and the glitter – you look really . . .' She struggled for the right word. 'Exceptional . . .'

8.20 p.m.

. . . about big issues

'Jade,' asked Cleo, ten minutes later, 'who is that gorgeous guy?'

'Kyle – you know the one from . . .'

'Not him, silly – the other one.'

'His mate – Angus Somebody or other.'

'Now he is real eye candy,' Cleo declared. 'I'm going to get him to dance.'

'Cleo! What's got into you?' Jade gasped. 'You can't just go up and grab him.'

'Watch me,' Cleo replied, sashaying across the room.

'Hi, I'm Cleo,' Jade heard her say in a far more husky voice than usual. 'You're Angus, right? Got any hip hop among that lot?'

Jade sighed. Even Cleo could get into the swing of it. I'll have to try harder, she told herself firmly.

8.40 p.m.

'He's still not here,' Allegra wailed, taking a can of cola from Jade's hand. 'Do you think he's ill? Should I text? Jade? Are you listening to me?'

'Wasn't it you who said girls had to play it cool?' Jade asked with a grin.

'There's cool and *cool*,' muttered Allegra.

8.50 p.m.

'I'm a star, I'm a raver, I'm a cool face-saver, I've got lip, I've got zip . . .'

Cleo belted out the lyrics of the latest BagHandlers hit as she danced.

'You've got the most amazing voice,' Angus told her. 'Where did you learn to sing like that?'

'It just happens,' Cleo told him. 'It's about the only thing I'm good at.'

'With a voice like that, you don't need to be good at anything else,' Angus said. 'Have you ever thought about cutting a disc?'

It's only flattery, Cleo told herself firmly. Just party talk. But it's nice.

'I've got lip, I've got zip, I'm the latest thing in hip . . .'

9.00 p.m.
Pulling tactics

'Hi Kyle – cool tracks!' Holly sashayed over to the disco, moving her hips in time to the beat and trying to remove the last traces of potato chip from her top teeth. 'Why don't you let Angus take over and come and dance?'

Kyle shook his head. 'I'm here to work.' He smiled. 'Not to party. Besides, he's dancing.'

'Angus! Kyle wants a break,' Holly called, trying not to notice the look of disappointment on Cleo's face.

'Sure,' Angus said. 'Go for it.'

Cool, Holly thought. Sorted.

9.10 p.m.
Watching from the sidelines, which is not a good place to be

This is the pits, thought Jade. Holly's bopping with Kyle, Cleo's glued to Angus's left hip, and Tansy is snogging Andy like she's in training for a lip marathon.

And I'm standing here cuddling a packet of Wotsits. Maybe I'll try out a couple of chat-up lines . . .

'I know what's happened!' Allegra cried in alarm, dashing up to Jade. 'The bell – no one will hear it over this noise! He's probably been standing out there for ages.'

She belted down the hall, zapped the bolt on the front door and wrenched it open.

'Good timing!' Two girls, one in a tight black leather miniskirt, the other wearing hipsters and a leopard-print top, burst into the hall, waving a couple of bottles. 'This is Jade's party, right?'

'Who the hell are . . .?' Allegra began and then stopped as another girl ran up the path. 'Brooke? Is this lot with you?'

'What's it to you? It's Jade's party – she said I could bring mates.'

Allegra was about to protest but another figure was coming up the path.

'Scott!' she cried with relief. 'What took you so long? Never mind, am I glad to see you – come on in. I'll get you a drink.'

Ten minutes later . . .

Feeling not quite right

'Brooke,' Jade said. 'Those two girls you came with . . .' She gestured across the room to where the girls were giggling over a mobile phone.

'Shelly and Dawn, you mean?' Brooke said.

'Well, aren't they the ones who've been giving you such hassle?'

Brooke shrugged. 'They've been really cool with me since I said they could come along tonight,' she said. 'They even bought the booze.'

'Booze?' Jade gulped. 'They can't . . .' She broke off as

she spotted Kyle pulling away from Holly and sauntering back to check his pile of CDs.

'Hang on,' she said. 'There's something I have to do.'

One minute later . . .

'Allegra,' asked Scott as she passed him a can of Appletise, 'where's Jade?'

'Oh, don't worry about . . .' she began, and then caught sight of her cousin. 'Actually, there she is.' She pointed across the darkened room. 'Over there, dancing with Kyle. Her new boyfriend.'

And then . . .

I've done it! Jade thought, giving it all she'd got as the beat of the music. I'm dancing with a guy, I look normal, he's smiling at me. So why don't I feel all those things that *Heaven Sent* says you should feel?

'So are you going to make music your career?' she asked Kyle, remembering the feature that said boys like talking about themselves.

He shook his head. 'If I get the grades, I'm going to uni to do politics with international studies,' he said.

'That's sounds pretty high-powered,' Jade said. 'So what do you want to be when you're done?'

'Well,' he began, 'I'd either like to . . .'

'Jade, I need to talk to you . . .' Scott was suddenly hovering at her side, shifting his weight from one foot to another.

'Not now, Scott,' she said. 'Sorry, Kyle – you were saying . . .'

'It's OK,' Kyle said, as the sound of the Hyperballistics faded away. 'I need a drink, anyway.'

'Well thank you so much, Scott Hamill!' Jade snapped as Kyle moved away. 'Just when I was getting it all together!'

It wasn't so much the look on Scott's face that made her feel guilty as the realisation that her heart hadn't been in it anyway.

9.25 p.m.
Bottling out

'Want a drink?' Brooke wielded a bottle in Jade's face.

'That's vodka!' Jade gasped.

'Oh, very observant,' sneered Brooke, taking a gulp and then pulling a face. 'Actually, I don't like it, but Shelley says . . .'

'You shouldn't have that stuff here,' Jade protested. 'And come to think of it, where is Shelley?'

9.26 p.m.

'Don't worry,' Allegra told Scott. 'Jade's not the angel everyone thinks she is, you know. Why don't we go in the kitchen and . . .'

'Not now,' Scott interrupted. 'I've got to talk to Tansy.'

9.30 p.m.
Calm before the storm

'You haven't heard a single word I've been saying, have you?' Andy stopped dancing, removed his specs and looked straight into Tansy's eyes. 'I've just told you that you're beautiful, sexy . . .'

Tansy smiled apologetically. 'Sorry,' she said. 'I'm not very good company, am I?'

'Look,' Andy said 'why don't we move into another room and just chill?'

He took her hand. 'And things?' he added.

9.32 p.m.
Pizza and problems

'Pizza's here!' yelled Allegra, cupping her hands to make herself heard above the babble of conversation. 'Can someone get the door?'

'We'll get it,' Andy called. He turned to Tansy and winked. 'That'll get us out of here!'

Tansy went ahead and opened the door.

'Here you are,' said the delivery boy. 'Ten pizzas, mixed order – ten more in the van. I'll only be a tick.'

Tansy passed the boxes to Andy and turned back. Instantly she was shoved to one side as three guys in sweatpants and T-shirts burst into the hall, shouting and chucking cans of beer at one another.

'Hey, you can't just . . .'

They pushed Andy out of the way as he tried to stop them and his shouts were drowned out by the thumping of the disco.

'Watcha, Shelley!' one of the boys called, staggering into the room.

'He's drunk,' Tansy gasped in horror.

'Hey, Dawn,' yelled another. 'Where's the booze, then?'

'Hi, Drew! It's all in the kitchen,' Dawn replied, slipping an arm through his. 'This way.'

The girls pushed open the door to the kitchen, wrenched open a cupboard and began grabbing bottles of wine.

'Not that – get the hard stuff, stupid!' spat one of the boys, and grabbed a bottle of Scotch from the shelf.

'Tansy, get Jade – fast!' gasped Andy. 'And get Kyle to kill the music.'

As Tansy ran along the hall, Scott appeared from the kitchen. 'Tansy, I need to . . .'

'Scott, quick – run out to the pizza man, and say we've got gatecrashers. Quick!'

Two minutes later . . .

'That's your problem,' muttered the delivery boy, dumping the remaining pizzas on the doorstep. 'Company policy – no interfering in domestic incidents. Sorry.'

'But they're taking stuff and . . .'

'So ring the police.' The boy sighed. 'Not my problem.'

9.40 p.m.
Help!

'Tansy, phone the police!' Scott shouted.

The three guys, armed with bottles, swaggered into the sitting room and slumped down on the two sofas.

'You can't do this!' shouted Kyle. 'Just get the hell out of here.'

'We'll go when we're ready,' spat the tallest of the boys, standing up and deliberately kicking one of the speakers, while taking huge swigs from the whiskey bottle. 'Oh, look – pizzas! We'll have some of those, Drew.'

Drew grabbed one of the boxes that Tansy had dumped on a chair, and ripped open the cardboard lid.

'Pepperoni – yuk!' He threw the pizza over his shoulder and it landed, topping side down, on the carpet. 'Hey guys – frisbees!'

Within seconds they were hurling pizzas round the room and passing the bottles between them. And then Drew threw up on the carpet.

'This is all your fault,' Jade sobbed at Brooke, tears streaming down her face. 'You should have known better than to invite those two.'

'I didn't know they'd do all this,' Brooke said, her voice shaking. 'Shelley just said the guys would come and get the booze and push off.'

'So you knew all along?' Jade was incredulous. 'You set me up. How could you do that?'

'I didn't have any choice,' Brooke blurted out.

'Oh sure you did!' Jade countered. 'Like saying no wasn't an option?'

'I was scared,' Brooke whispered. 'Dead scared.'

9.45 p.m.
Getting assertive

'The police are on their way!' Tansy ran into the room and then stopped dead, her face pale at the sight of the pool of vomit and the reeling Drew.

'We've got to ring your parents,' Jade urged Allegra, ignoring Brooke, who was sobbing in a corner.

'No!' cried Allegra, her eyes wide with fear. 'They'll kill us. We've got time to clear up . . .'

'Hey, guys, we've got to get the hell out of here!' Shelley shouted. 'They've called the cops.'

'Not before we gesh nuvver bockle . . .' one of the guys cried, slurring his speech as he staggered to his feet and lurched towards the kitchen.

'Stuff that for an idea!' Cleo marched up to him and barred his way. 'If you don't clear off, the only bottle you're getting will be smashed over your head!'

Jade looked at Holly. Holly stared at Tansy. 'What's happened to her?' she breathed. 'It never said anything about a change of personality on the hair-dye packet.'

9.46 p.m.

'Come on, you guys – beat it!' Dawn dragged Drew to his feet and headed for the door, with Shelley and the other guys close behind her.

'Thanks for the booze!' the tall one yelled, crashing into the doorpost as he waved a bottle above his head. 'Nice one!'

'And where do you think you're going?' Jade demanded, grabbing Brooke's arm as she tried to leave.

'The police . . .' Brooke began.

'. . . will be very interested in your information,' Jade retorted. 'You're not going anywhere.'

9.50 p.m.
Operation clean-up

'OK, guys,' Kyle shouted, clapping his hands. 'Angus and I will clear the puke – the rest of you get cloths, water, disinfectant and the vacuum cleaner. This is going to be one long job.'

'He's very masterful, isn't he?' Holly murmured to Cleo.

'But not nearly as sexy as Angus,' added Cleo. 'Poor Jade, what a party – she looks gutted.'

10.00 p.m.
Don't shoot the messenger

'Tansy,' Scott began, dipping a scrubbing brush into a bucket of Fairy liquid. 'I know this isn't the best time . . .'

'You can say that again,' Tansy replied, wiping cheese and bits of tomato off the walls.

'But I saw Patrick this evening.'

Tansy dropped her J-cloth and stared at him.

'That's why I was late getting here,' he went on. 'He and Felicity came to my house to say hi to my folks and to apologise for the missed dinner date. We talked about you.'

'That was so not on,' Tansy began. 'He was a complete asshole and . . .'

'I know, he told me,' Scott said.

'He admitted it?'

Scott nodded. 'I wasn't going to hang around,' he admitted. 'But he kind of cornered me and asked if I'd be seeing you, and I said yes and . . . well, the thing is, he's leaving for the States early tomorrow morning.'

'Good,' said Tansy shortly.

'So he gave me this. For you.' He put his hand in his trouser pocket and pulled out a somewhat crumpled envelope.

Tansy stared at it, but made no move to take it.

'He said that he knew he couldn't make you read it, but he made me promise to give it to you,' Scott finished. 'I've done that. The rest is up to you.' He sighed. 'How do you get salami off TV screens?'

10.02 p.m.
Crunch time

'You won't say anything to the police, will you?' Brooke begged, wiping a cloth half-heartedly over the door frame.

'Why shouldn't I?' Jade retorted. 'You're the one who landed us in this mess.'

'I didn't know, honestly,' Brooke repeated, fear in her eyes. 'All I knew was that Shell and Dawn were going to try to steal some booze.'

'And you were up for that?' Jade scoffed, shouting over the noise of the vacuum cleaner that Cleo was manoeuvring round the room.

'You'd have done the same thing if it had been you they were threatening,' Brooke stormed. 'Like when I tried to grab your mobile phone last Monday . . .'

'*What?*' Jade was almost speechless. 'I thought you just fell . . .'

'That was me trying to cover up for getting it wrong yet again,' Brooke said miserably. 'Then they said I had to steal something from a shop and when I gave them the sweets, they said I was a wimp and it should have been make-up and stuff from a department store.'

'But Brooke, why did you do it?' Jade stressed every word as if Brooke was hard of hearing. 'They're a couple of girls – they were hardly going to beat you up.'

'Oh yeah, well that shows what you know!' Brooke began to cry.

'Anyway, it wasn't me I was worried about. It was

my gran.' She took a deep breath. 'I used to live with my gran, right,' she said. 'And these girls lived on the same estate – Frenchfields?'

Jade shuddered inwardly. Frenchfields was Dunchester's worst area. She'd never been there but she'd read about it in the local paper. It seemed like there was always trouble going on.

'They found out my dad was in prison, and that's when they started getting me to do stuff. And when I said no – cos at first I did – they threw a brick through my gran's window. One day they pushed a burning duster through our door.'

'That's awful,' Jade gasped, pausing in her endeavours to clean up. 'But I still don't get why they weren't caught.'

'You don't go running to the police round where I used to live,' Brooke shrugged. 'You'd be asking for trouble. So Gran just decided to move away. That's when I went into foster care and came to West Green.'

Jade began to feel a bit guilty. 'But if you'd told someone . . .' she persisted.

'Jade,' Brooke said, very softly and very firmly. 'You live in this lovely house, right? You've got a proper family and loads of friends. Don't tell me what you would or wouldn't do if you had lived my life. Cos you don't have a flipping clue.'

10.05 p.m.

The truth, the whole truth . . .

'So just what happened here?' the police officer asked.

'These guys . . . took the booze . . . throwing food . . . came in when the pizza man . . .'

'OK, OK, one at a time,' he said. 'First of all, which one of you lives here?'

'Me,' said Allegra.

'And me,' added Jade.

'And where are your parents?'

'Out,' they said in unison.

'And you've called them, of course? You haven't? Get on the phone right now. What do you think it's going to do to them if they arrive home to find a squad car parked outside?'

10.15 p.m.

Confession down the line

'No, we're all fine. No, no one's been hurt. The house is fine – well, almost. Sort of. Sorry.'

Jade put the phone down and turned to Allegra.

'Well?' asked her cousin.

'She wasn't too bad about it,' Jade said.

'The bad will come later,' Allegra said, sighing. 'With my mother, it always does.'

10.20 p.m.

Questions, questions . . .

'And no one knows the gatecrashers?' The police officer didn't look convinced.

'No,' said Jade. 'But we know the girls who tipped them off.'

'Jade . . .' Brooke hissed.

'It's OK,' Jade said. 'Officer, can we talk in private?'

10.22 p.m.

'She's terrified,' Jade told the officer. 'All I know is that they're called Shelley and Dawn and they live on Frenchfields estate. But if they think Brooke told you . . .'

'Leave it with me,' the officer replied with a smile. 'And thanks for the description of the lads – I think I know where I'll find them. You've been very sensible.'

'I don't suppose,' asked Jade, 'that when my aunt and uncle get back, you could persuade them to agree with you?'

Two minutes later . . .

Police versus parents

'Oh my God!' Jade's aunt stood, hand on heart, in the doorway, surveying the room. The carpet was wet where Kyle and Angus had scrubbed away all traces of vomit, the walls still had stains where food had landed, and the whole place stank of alcohol.

'Jade, how could you let this happen? Allegra - never again will I let you . . .'

'Hang on a moment, madam,' the police officer said. 'In all probability, it's not the fault of these kids. When thugs decided to gatecrash there's very little anyone can do. And your youngsters kept their cool - they called us and they've cleaned up. Well, after a fashion.'

'I'm really sorry, Aunt Paula,' Jade began.

'We all are,' Tansy cut in. 'But honestly, we had nothing to do with it.'

'And Jade tried ever so hard to get rid of them,' added Scott. 'In fact, she risked life and limb.'

'OK, OK,' Jade's uncle cut in, a faint smile on this lips. 'We get the point. No one is hurt and that's the main thing.'

'I suppose,' his wife said, turning the police officer, 'that you're going to tell us that it's our fault for going out and leaving them in the first place.'

The policeman grinned. 'I wouldn't dream of it, madam,' he replied. 'I've got three teenagers of my own at home. If you had stayed home, they would have gone out. You can't win, can you?'

10.40 p.m.

'Sorry the party was spoiled, guys.' Kyle paused on his way to load his gear into the van. 'But I've got an idea –

we're playing for our college disco in a couple of months' time. Why don't I get you a few tickets? Make up for not getting what you paid for tonight?'

'That would be great,' Holly breathed.

'Brilliant,' added Tansy.

'Will Angus be there?' asked Cleo.

'Of course he will,' said Kyle, laughing. 'Where I go, he goes. Always.'

If he meant what I think he meant, thought Jade with a jolt, I've been wasting my time trying to pretend, and Holly's in for one huge shock.

10.45 p.m.

'Can't wait, can you?' Holly said nudging Jade. 'For the college do – loads of fit guys, not that I need one now I've got Kyle but you could . . .'

'I don't actually think that you have got Kyle,' Jade ventured. 'I mean, if everywhere he goes, Angus goes too.'

'Well, he would, they're in the band together and . . . oh no. You don't think – I mean, they can't be?'

'I rather think,' nodded Jade, 'they might be.'

Oh sugar plum fairies, thought Holly.

10.50 p.m.

'Do you think,' Cleo asked Holly eagerly as she waited for her mum to pick her up, 'that Angus fancied me?'

'I should think that is highly unlikely.' Holly sighed.

Cleo's face fell. 'It was the hair, wasn't it?' she murmured miserably.

'No, silly,' replied Holly. 'It was the fact that you're a girl.'

11.30 p.m.

Later at home, locked in the bathroom

Tansy unfolded the letter and perched on the edge of the bath.

Dear Tansy,

I guess if you are reading these words you haven't torn up my letter in disgust, though I wouldn't blame you if you had. I was a jerk yesterday and I'm sorry. I could spin you a yarn, say that having slept on it I'm totally overjoyed to have found you and that I want us to live happily ever after. But I respect you too much to kid you. I was so scared when you turned up; and I explained why. Your mum and I did some dumb things that summer fifteen years ago and what I want to say to you now – as your father (if that's what I am and frankly, I still can't get my head around that) – is never, ever mess with drugs or alcohol or guys you hardly know. Clarity was lucky and so are you: she got a great daughter and you clearly have a mum who is a much better parent than I could ever be. But it could have turned out much worse. I guess we won't be seeing one another any more – it's only in the movies that the dream endings happen. Be happy and don't keep looking back. The future is much more interesting.

Stay safe, Patrick

11.35 p.m.

'Tansy? Are you OK?' Clarity banged on the bathroom door.

'Just coming,' Tansy shouted.

She took one final look at the letter, folded it and began to stuff it in her pocket. She paused and looked at it one more time.

Then she tore it into tiny fragments and flushed it down the loo. It was over. She'd met the man who was probably her father and that's all he was. A man. She didn't have any feelings for him, she didn't need him.

She had all she needed right here.

'You're not feeling ill, are you?' her mother called anxiously.

'No, Mum,' she said, smiling as she opened the door. 'I'm feeling absolutely fine.'

11.40 p.m.

On the way to bed

'I was really scared,' Holly admitted to her mother as she sipped a hot chocolate. 'It's put me off parties for life.'

'Can I have that in writing?' her aunt requested.

SUNDAY

8.30 a.m.
Rude awakenings

'Holly, out of bed, quickly!' Holly's mum burst into her bedroom and pulled the duvet off her bed.

'Mum!' Holly groaned, yanking it back again. 'It's Sunday.'

'You've got ten minutes to be up and dressed,' her mother declared, ignoring her protests. 'We've got people coming to view the house.' She surveyed the chaos in Holly's room with distaste. 'And get this cleared up,' she ordered. 'We don't want people being put off.'

'Mum,' Holly said, yawning, 'once they've seen the broken boiler and the damp on the study ceiling, I hardly think a couple of pairs of my trainers and the odd sweatshirt is going to bother them.'

10.00 a.m.
Postmortem

'I still say it was Jade's fault,' Allegra insisted as the family sat over a late breakfast. 'If she hadn't got all matey with Brooke Sylvester, none of this would have happened.'

'I felt sorry for her,' Jade protested. 'How was I to know that she was going to set us up?'

'If you'd had half a brain . . .' Allegra began.

'Stop it right now, you two,' Jade's uncle declared, slapping the *Sunday Times* down on the table. 'What's done is done. The main thing is that . . .' He paused as the front door bell shrilled. 'Now who on earth can that be on a Sunday morning? Jade, be a dear and go and see.'

10.05 a.m.
Explanations

'This is my Uncle David – and this is Paula, my aunt.'

Jade stood back as a tall woman with a mane of chestnut hair scooped into a tortoiseshell clip burst into the room. Trailing behind her, with a face like thunder, was Brooke.

'Mrs Webb,' the woman said, holding out a hand, 'I do apologise for bursting in on you, but I had to come and try to make amends for what my daughter has done.' She sighed. 'I'm Alice Sylvester,' she explained. 'Brooke's mother.'

'Foster mother, you mean?' queried Jade, noting the dark lines under the woman's eyes.

Mrs Sylvester closed her eyes for a second and then turned to Brooke. 'So you're back on that story, are you, Brooke? And what else have you told them? Was it the father in prison? The mum in a mental hospital? The baby sister at death's door?'

'You mean,' gasped Jade, 'those things you told me

weren't true? What about your gran and the bricks through her window? What about Frenchfields estate?'

'That's a new one,' Alice remarked. 'Brooke lives with me and her father in Blackwater Road.'

Jade blinked. Now she really was confused. Was anything Brooke said really true?

Mrs Sylvester paused, biting a fingernail. 'I'm afraid I've got some very serious stuff to tell you,' she said, turning to the Webbs.

'Allegra, Jade – upstairs,' ordered Jade's aunt.

'No!' Mrs Sylvester held up a hand. 'I don't mean to be rude but I think they ought to hear this. I don't know which one of you invited Brooke to your party . . .'

'Me,' said Jade. 'Those girls were being so horrid to her and . . .'

'Those girls? The other members of her gang, you mean?'

'No,' Jade burst out. 'You've got it wrong – they were hassling her and she was scared . . .'

'Brooke, tell them,' ordered her mother.

'Do I have to?' Brooke murmured, suddenly looking more like ten than fifteen.

'Yes,' her mother insisted.

'It was a set-up,' she said, sniffing, looking at Jade and chewing her lip. 'They pretend to be bullying me, I act like the wet and wimpy one, take the stuff, and we share the proceeds.'

Jade gasped, trying to get her head round what she was hearing.

'But the sweets – what was the point of taking sweets?' she asked.

Brooke flushed. 'They wanted fags,' she admitted. 'I showed you the sweets, and stuffed the fags into my pocket.'

'There's more, I'm afraid,' Mrs Sylvester went on. 'Brooke took these from your house.' She pulled a polythene bag from her pocket.

'That's my bangle!' Allegra gasped. 'And my house keys!'

'It wasn't me – I swear to you, it wasn't me!' Brooke burst into tears. 'You have to believe me. I wouldn't do stuff like that. Shelley took them – she and Dawn went upstairs, saying they needed the loo.'

'So how come they were in your pocket?' her mother demanded.

Suddenly, Jade had had enough. She didn't like the way Mrs Sylvester was laying into Brooke in front of them all, and she didn't like the self-satisfied expression on her face. She was about to say something when her uncle, David, cut into the conversation.

'Mrs Sylvester, I appreciate your coming to see us. And thank you for bringing back Allegra's things. I'm sure that had nothing to do with Brooke.'

Jade couldn't miss the fleeting expression of pure gratitude that crossed Brooke's tear-stained face.

'She never used to be like this,' Brooke's mother admitted. 'It's only since she got in with that crowd.'

'And at least she owned up,' David went on.

'Only when her father told her that he'd spotted her leaving the house with a couple of drunken louts,' her mother said, sniffing.

'Well, it took courage, didn't it?' said David, smiling. 'Thank you, Brooke – and if you take my advice, you'll steer well clear of Shelley and her friends.'

Brooke didn't say anything, but she nodded and wiped her eyes with the back of her hand.

'You're very forgiving,' Mrs Sylvester said, and it seemed to Jade that she was pretty miffed that there hadn't been an all-out bust up.

'I just remember what it's like to be a teenager.' David laughed. 'Just!'

11.30 a.m.

'I know what you're all thinking,' Jade said. 'If I hadn't interfered, none of this would have happened.'

'Jade,' encouraged her aunt. 'You've got a kind heart. You weren't to know the girl was a con artist.'

'Just remember, though,' her uncle added, 'you can't put the whole world to rights single-handed. Sometimes, you just have to let people sort themselves out.'

12.15 p.m.

'Tansy? It's Holly. Isn't it a tragedy? I mean, can you imagine anything more unfair, more awful . . .'

'I know,' Tansy agreed. 'Poor Jade.'

'Poor Jade? What about poor me?' demanded Holly.

'Well, it wasn't your party and it wasn't your house that got trashed,' Tansy reasoned.

'I'm not talking about all that,' Holly scoffed. 'I'm talking about Kyle.'

'What about him? Has he asked Jade out?'

Holly sighed. 'What planet are you on?' she demanded. 'Kyle's not asking anyone out. Well, none of us anyway. He's gay.'

'I knew Angus was but Kyle? I mean, he's such a hunk. What a waste.'

12.30 p.m.
Sorted!

'Oh my God, oh my God – Jade, he's rung. Scott. He's asked me bowling. I'm useless at bowling. But then that's good, isn't it? I mean, it'll make him feel macho if I'm useless. But then, if I'm useless, he might not ask me again. How should I play it? You have to help me.'

Jade listened to Allegra's breathless tirade and shook her head. 'From now on,' she said smiling sweetly, 'I'm letting people sort themselves out.'

12.35 p.m.
Father in charge

'Right, coats on everyone,' cried Mr Vine. 'We're going to see a property.'

'But Rupert,' protested Holly's mum, 'the lamb's in the oven and the apple crumble . . .'

'Do you want to move or not?' he asked.

'I'll just turn the oven down,' she murmured. 'Holly. Car. Now.'

12.45 p.m.

'Mum, you know the TV show you cancelled? Well, ring them up tomorrow and say we'll do it, OK?'

'But darling, you said you hated the idea,' her mother protested.

'The old me hated it,' corrected Cleo. 'The new me thinks it might be a laugh.'

Diana eyed her closely. 'Are you sure you're feeling OK? No one spiked your drink last night?'

'The only thing spiked round here is my hair,' grinned Cleo. 'I just discovered that I'm not boring after all.'

1.10 p.m.

'Dad,' exclaimed Holly, 'you said we were going to look at a house.'

'I said,' corrected her father, 'that we were going to look at a property.'

'But Rupert,' his wife added anxiously, 'we are standing outside a windmill.'

2.30 p.m.

Tansy's mother was flicking through a gardening catalogue and Tansy was surfing the net in the hope of downloading a history essay when the bell rang.

'It's Trudie,' Tansy's mother said, peering through the sitting room window.

'Right,' murmured Tansy.

'And Kyle,' added her mother.

'Kyle?' Tansy gasped, zapping the Save button and leaving the computer. 'Oh good – I need to ask him a few questions.'

'Do your homework,' her mother said, laughing.

'There are other things of interest on this earth apart from homework,' Tansy replied. 'And one of them is on the doorstep.'

2.45 p.m.

'But that windmill is very historic,' Mr Vine remarked over a late lunch. 'It stands on the edge of the battlefield where the Roundheads . . .'

'Rupert, watch my lips,' said his wife. 'I want

something modern, something that is easy to clean, light, airy, and . . .' She hesitated, searching for the right word.

'Normal?' suggested Holly.

'Precisely,' agreed her mother.

'You are both,' he said, sighing, 'totally soulless.'

'Better than totally mad,' murmured Holly.

2.55 p.m.

'The thing is,' Kyle began, as his mother and Clarity talked nineteen to the dozen about the merits of growing a bamboo forest on the roof of Barclaycard's office, 'I wondered if you had Cleo's phone number.'

'Cleo? You want her phone number?'

'Yes,' muttered Kyle. 'What's so wrong with that?'

'But you can't. I mean, Holly said . . . why do you want it?'

'It's not for me, it's for Angus,' he said. 'Anyway, what are you – her guardian angel?'

To her relief, Tansy saw he was grinning. 'No, it's nothing, I just thought – her mobile is 07781 . . .' She dictated the number as Kyle scribbled on the back of his hand with a roller pen.

'And Angus wants to see Cleo?' she asked again. 'And you don't mind?'

'Mind? Why on earth would I mind?'

'That's good, then.' Tansy smiled. 'Want a drink?'

3.30 p.m.

'Angus fancies Cleo, so he can't be gay, and Kyle doesn't care, so that proves it,' Tansy told Holly, holding her mobile phone on one shoulder while she finished downloading her homework. 'Sorted.'

5.00 p.m.

'Your father has something to say to you,' Holly's mum told her. 'Haven't you, Rupert?'

'Have I, dear? Oh yes. Science.'

Here we go, Holly said to herself. Here comes the lecture.

'You are clearly not interested in science, and you are clearly very good at art and English,' said her dad. 'So I will have a word with your Year Tutor and see if you can take single science and do graphics and applied art and design instead.'

Holly's heart soared. 'You mean it? And you're not cross?'

'Actually,' her mum cut in, 'we are both furious.'

'Oh,' said Holly.

'With ourselves, silly,' her mother said. 'We should have realised you were struggling and done something about it. Besides, you're old enough now to make your own choices.'

Holly hugged her mum and kissed the top of her father's head. 'I don't suppose,' she asked cheekily, 'you could put that last bit in writing and sign it? Just in case you forget what you've just said.'

'Holly,' said her father. 'Don't push it.'

8.00 p.m.

'Me?' gasped Cleo. 'You want me?'

Her heart pounded and she gripped the handset till her knuckles turned white. He's going to ask me out, she thought. I've died and gone to heaven.

'Want me to what?'

Kiss you? Snog you senseless?

'Sing? With your band?' She swallowed hard. 'Well, yes, I love singing, and I guess if I could persuade my parents . . . at least you and I would get see one another loads.' She half-closed her eyes and pretended Angus was right beside her. 'What? You and Kyle are what? Oh.'

Cleo Greenway, you are a fool, she told herself.

'No, no of course not. I have no problem with that. None at all.'

If you don't count the broken heart, she sighed, dropping the handset on the table.

9.30 p.m.

'I thought he might phone you,' Tansy's mother said as she cleared away the supper dishes.

'Who?' Tansy asked.

'Patrick,' she admitted. 'Before he left. Stupid of me, I guess.'

Should I tell her about the letter? Tansy mused.

'I was stupid,' her mum went on. 'Just for a moment, back there at the hotel when you told me that you'd found Pongo, I dreamed of a happy ending. Then you mentioned his wife and . . .'

'Mum,' said Tansy. 'It's only in the movies that the dream endings happen. We have to be happy and stop looking back. The future is much more interesting.'

Her mother gave a hug. 'Sometimes, Tansy Meadows, you are very wise,' she murmured.

'Now, that I *do* get from you,' Tansy told her. 'I love you, Mum.'